MW01106857

Running Home

Jennifer Charron Ward

FERNE PRESS

Running Home
Copyright © 2009 by Jennifer Charron Ward
Printed in Canada

Cover illustration by Megan D. Wellman

Summary: The story of an unwanted puppy, and how he finds the family and home of his dreams.

Library of Congress Cataloging-in-Publication Data
Ward, Jennifer Charron (1968 -)
Running Home / Jennifer Charron Ward – First Edition
ISBN-13: 978-1-933916-37-8
1. Juvenile fiction. 2. Adopting dogs. 3. Paranormal. 4. Animal rescue.
I. Ward, Jennifer Charron II. Running Home
Library of Congress Control Number: 2009920323

FERNE PRESS

Ferne Press is an imprint of Nelson Publishing & Marketing
366 Welch Road, Northville, MI 48167
www.nelsonpublishingandmarketing.com
(248) 735-0418

Dedication

This book is dedicated to all the people who have rescued or adopted a pet, especially to my friend Anna Olech who has spent her life saving homeless dogs. It is written in honor of my grandparents, Clare and Trudy Charron.

Acknowledgments

I would like to acknowledge my husband, Larry, and my children, Jake and Josie, for being so patient and keeping their sense of humor. I would also like to acknowledge my mother, Julie Hanson, for giving me her unwavering support and love. Thanks to my publisher, Marian Nelson, for accepting this manuscript, and to my editor, Kris Yankee, for teaching me how to write. Thanks to my aunt, Sue Davis, for her enthusiasm and endless resources. And, special thanks and love to my nephew, Nicholas Doherty, for reading my early story and providing so many valuable ideas and suggestions.

Prologue

Trudy

Just after the start of the New Year, when the days were dark and the weather was dreary, a dying woman made a request to the heavens. It was an unusual request, but the woman felt it was warranted and that it should be given special consideration. It's not that she was brilliant or famous, and she certainly didn't have a direct channel to God. She was simply a devoted wife and mother, and most of her friends regarded her as virtuous. But the woman disagreed, and felt restless and discontented. She had made a mistake that weighed so heavily on her heart, she couldn't bear to die until it was reversed. Although it hadn't been considered a crime, the old woman knew that she had done nothing short of neglecting and discarding someone she had promised to care for. She couldn't seem to escape the neverending reminder that she had hurt someone who loved her unconditionally. So in trying to rectify her sin in the form of a prayer, she asked for a favor. The old woman requested that her loved one be brought back to life, so that he may have a second chance at a world she so selfishly took from him. She asked that he end up with someone who would care for him and cherish him until death do them part.

And so that summer on a small farm in Michigan, unbeknownst to the old lady, a litter of German shepherd puppies was born and her prayer was answered.

Chapter One

An Unnamed Dog

I knew something was wrong.

Mama was nervous, and Alice and Ben acted funny. It was as though they were saying goodbye. But that was ridiculous. My siblings and I were Mama's children, and Alice and Ben were our owners. The farm was our home, and Mama had promised to love us forever. Although it was only the fifth week of my life, I was the happiest I'd ever been . . . until today.

Alice stood in the center of the room and twisted a window rag in her hands. She had just finished wiping nose slobber off the glass. Sighing, she shook her head. "Okay, babies, I think we're ready for Dumb Head."

Ben sat in the wicker chair, staring at a ball that he rolled in his hands. He gave Alice a funny look, and she started to cry. Dropping the rag to the floor, she buried her face in her hands. I crawled behind the toy basket, while my siblings continued to play. Mama still slept in the kitchen.

"We still have two weeks to go, Al," Ben said in his calmest voice. "You go through this every time, and you always end up okay in the end. Just remember, we need the money. The puppies will be fine."

"I know, I know. I just don't like that man. He's so . . . Well, I don't believe he gives a rat's rump. They're so tiny and . . . I don't know." Alice sniffled. "I just have a bad feeling about him."

"I know," Ben reassured, "but no one else would ever give

us the kind of money Mr. Cooper's willin' to. Remember the last time we tried to sell 'em ourselves? We ended up losin' money in the end on vet bills, food, whatever. This guy gave us the daddy for free, is takin' 'em to his own vet, gettin' 'em out in six weeks, and tellin' us they'll have good homes. Al, we could never do that. And, one hundred dollars a dog besides? You'll be okay, I promise. We really need that five hundred dollars."

Alice blew her nose. It honked loudly. "Yes, I know. I just can't face him today. Mama and I will be in the kitchen."

The door creaked open, then banged shut. I opened my eyes and peeked around the basket to see Ben slumped sadly in the chair. He put the ball in his pocket and lit a pipe, watching as my siblings rolled and wrestled on the floor. Shaking the flame from his match, he leaned back and crossed his legs. Suddenly he stood, setting his pipe in the ashtray.

"Where is . . . ?" His eyelids squinted, while his gaze darted from one corner of the porch to another. "Oh, there you are, you big moose." He sighed and strolled over to my hiding spot. "You gave me quite a scare for a second." He picked me up and ruffled my head. Then, he smiled and changed his voice to a whisper. "Hey, Moosie, how would you like something all to yourself? I found it out by the road this mornin' and wasn't sure any of you were big enough for it." He set me down. "But seein' that you've grown faster than the rest, it might be all right." He pulled the ball out of his pocket. It was bright pink and shiny and about the size of a big tomato. "See? It squeaks." As he handed it to me, a funny noise blew out. I wagged my tail and took the ball. It was hard to grasp, but I hung on. "There you go, boy. Just give it a few weeks."

Ben turned toward the window and groaned. "Oh, look who the devil just dragged in. You little ones be on your best behavior and just ignore what this idiot has to say. He's not a bad guy, like old Alice thinks, he's just doin' his business." With that, Ben clambered out the door hollering hello to Dumb Head.

Dumb Head followed Ben onto the porch. He was a short, stout man and had to look up when he spoke. His shirt was silky blue with a button missing. He wore a brown and purple striped tie that draped over his rounded belly where a yellow stain half hid. There was a thin ring of hair around his head, and his skin glowed red with sunburn. His nostrils were huge, and there was a dried booger that flapped and wiggled with every exhalation. He had thick tortoiseshell glasses that he pushed toward his nose repeatedly, and he talked with his hands.

"Well, Farmer Ben, these puppies look like they've faired well enough."

Ben replied politely, "We've sure tried our best to keep 'em growin' and eatin' and what not. Alice, she does a fine job when it comes to raisin' these little stinkers, but it's wearin' on her this time. Same with ol' Mama. She's not very happy these days. Seems awfully tired to me."

"Oh, they'll pull through, especially the dog. I saw her in the window, barking at me. She looks darned strong." He cleared his throat. "Dogs don't have feelings anyway. It's all the same to them." He cleared his throat again and horked up something that he buried in his handkerchief. He stuck the rag back in his pocket and started to move toward us. "Here, let me see one of these critters." He wiped his hands on his pants and leaned over to pick up my sister. Ben suddenly looked nervous and jolted forward.

"Wait," interjected Ben, as he blocked Dumb Head. "The

puppies are still afraid of strangers, and maybe you should give 'em the two weeks to get bigger before you start handlin' them."

"Horse hockey." Dumb Head practically shoved Ben aside to get to my sister and in doing so, he stepped on my tail.

I cried out, and Dumb Head jumped high into the air, holding his hand to his chest. "Jiminy Crickets!" he yelled. When his foot came back down, he slipped on my ball, which made him lose his balance and fall into the screen door. As the screen ripped from its frame, Dumb Head's chunky body toppled through the doorway toward the driveway. He bumped his head on the way out, knocking his glasses off of his nose. "Ahh, garsh-dangat!" he sputtered, as his bottom hit the ground. He sat stunned momentarily, then checked his head and his fingers. The other hand reached down to search for his glasses.

"Don't mind those; I'll get 'em," said Ben, rushing to help him. Although Ben acted nice, I could tell he was annoyed. He helped Dumb Head back through the door, and then picked his glasses off the floor. Ignoring the damaged screen, Ben scooped me up and looked at my tail. Alice and Mama had come from the kitchen to see what all the noise was about. Ben handed me to Alice while Dumb Head finished cleaning his glasses. "Here, Al, make sure he's okay," Ben whispered, then turned to Dumb Head who had begun to fiddle with the door. "Don't worry about that, sir. It's easy to fix. You've done us enough favors, and we appreciate each and every one of 'em."

Dumb Head straightened his tie and touched his head one more time. He pushed up his glasses and cleared his throat. "Okay, Ben, everything looks good here." More throat clearing. "I'll be back to pick up the dogs on August first. I already have people interested, so they won't be hard to get rid of."

"Sounds good, sir. We'll have 'em ready." Ben looked like he wanted to say something else, but hesitated. He tried again and stammered out the words. "Um, maybe Alice and I could have the names of the people who buy the puppies. You know, maybe we could visit 'em sometime."

From Alice's arms, I listened closely for Dumb Head's reply. Alice stood still and turned her ear toward the door. The men had already gone outside.

"Nope. Not good business, Farmer Ben. These people want pets of their own. They don't want anyone checking up on them. They want to feel that they can do whatever they want with their own property, if you catch my drift."

Ben didn't argue. "Fair enough. See you in two weeks."

I heard Dumb Head's car fire up and drive away. Alice resumed her crying and set me down.

As I looked around at my house and my yard, I realized I wouldn't be here much longer. I would probably never get to run around here like Mama or do chores with Ben. The days when I would wake up and see Mama's face or hear her comforting words were over. My life as I knew it was coming to an end, a chapter of my life that I thought would last forever.

Chapter Two

Trudy

The old lady grew weaker. She didn't expect to last much longer. Her illness had taken its toll on her body, and she was tired. The walks that used to please her no longer did, and friends rarely made her smile. She thought back to the times when stepping out of bed wasn't a task or eating breakfast didn't make her short of breath. But things had changed as things always do. She was nearing the end and didn't expect an easy transition to heaven. She wasn't even sure if that's where she would go. After all, she wasn't always a good person.

On the morning of August first, the woman felt especially sickened and remorseful. She had been startled awake by a disturbing dream. In fact, it was so upsetting that the woman was sure she had cried out in her sleep. Pushing the dampened covers off of her body, she slowly moved her legs to the side of the bed and paused to say a morning prayer. She reminded God of her previous request and hoped that he had not forgotten.

An Unnamed Dog

I had a horrible dream.

The late afternoon sun shone through puffs of fair-weather clouds and warmed my fur. Leaves from above shimmered a bright mix of oranges, reds, and golds, while those on the ground tossed about playfully. I sat stretched out on a freshly cut carpet of grass, staring at my reflection in a pond. I noticed that I was a full-grown dog. My head was mostly black except for some tan that ran from my eyebrows down to the tip of my nose. My ears stood perky and sharp. My neck was light tan as well as my legs, and I had a coal-black coat on my back and tail. I looked across the water to thick fields and dense forest, hearing bullfrogs croak among the reeds. When I turned my head toward the road, there was a house that sat overlooking the grounds. It was a white, two-story, wood-sided farm house with lots of windows. A brick chimney jutted out from the dark green shingled roof, puffing smoke into the air. As I studied my surroundings, I felt happy and content. My stomach was full, and I was loved.

A woman, who looked to be my owner, relaxed in a patio chair. She read a book and sipped lemonade. She was thin and pretty with a slightly pronounced nose, dark blond wavy hair, and bright blue eyes. She had peppy red lipstick that lined her upturned mouth and straight white teeth. Her dress was stylish and colorful, pressed and tucked to perfection. Her house slippers were flat and beaded, and they matched the pattern of her wide-brimmed hat. The familiar scent of her perfume wafted past my nose and blended with the rose garden just beyond.

The woman clearly waited for someone to come home, for she kept peering over her book at the empty dirt road. Every now and then, she looked at me and blew a kiss. "Hi, my beautiful Thor. What would I do without my boy?" It was as though I was the most important thing in her life.

After what seemed like hours, she got up and walked toward me. She held her hand out to touch my head, and I felt so excited. I wagged my tail and rolled onto my back. Then suddenly, she started to cry. Her lovely face twisted as tears flowed over her milky white skin. Little by little she changed, as her cries turned to sobs. The mouth that was so perfect just moments before became widened and deformed. She yelled, "Goodbye, Thor! I'm sorry, my boy!" As her voice intensified, screeching howls forced their way out of her throat, and a sickening liquid dripped from her eyes. With each drop, more of her features disappeared until they were gone completely. I stood up and backed away. But she continued to move forward, screaming my name even though she no longer had a face. "Thor! Thor! I'm sorry, my beautiful dog. I'm sorry, my beautiful Thor!" The words erupted from deep within her neck, while she clambered along the grass, dragging her disintegrated feet. "Thor, Thor, come here, boy. I'm sorry."

I couldn't imagine what she was sorry about. She seemed to be someone I loved very much. I wasn't frightened of her until she began to fall apart, and then I became terrified. As I backed further toward the pond, I realized I was crying and woke up.

I continued to cry even after I was fully awake. For some reason, the nightmare had a powerful effect on me. My muscles stiffened, and my heart pounded. What finally comforted me was seeing my siblings close by.

When I realized Dumb Head was taking us that day, I felt nervous. I didn't panic, because Ben told us he wasn't a bad guy, and I trusted Ben. But, he and Alice acted strange again. Ben was silent all morning, and Alice went into another fit of crying and couldn't stop. She kept picking us up, drenching us with her tears.

"Oh, Moosie, I'm so sorry," she said as she held me to her face and slobbered in my ear. By midmorning, I was tired of it. She reminded me of the lady in my dream. Her face turned puffy, and she was ugly with all of her whining. Even Mama didn't do that, and she was my real mother.

Later on, we heard his car. Dumb Head's vehicle had a distinct sound, and his muffler was as loud as Ben's lawn mower. My stomach felt sick, and my heart raced. I didn't want to go, but I knew Ben and Alice wouldn't change their minds. I wished at that moment I could make myself homely and worthless; that I could lose all my fur and make my eyes bloodshot and scary. I wanted Dumb Head to say, "Oh, I don't think I can take this one. He's too big, besides he's bald and there's something wrong with his eyes." But Dumb Head walked up the drive and shook Ben's hand. He gave Alice a condescending nod and smiled through the porch screen where we sat huddled together.

"Well, they look good, Farmer Ben," he said enthusiastically, rubbing his hands together. "You'll hear from me as soon as they all get sold. Then I'll bring you that big fat check I promised."

Alice and Ben came solemnly onto the porch and took us one by one out to Dumb Head's car. Ben's nose was red, and I could tell he wanted to cry. Holding us extra tight, they placed us in the crates that Dumb Head had set up in the back. There were no blankets or toys, so Alice put one of each in our crates as her tears dripped onto the rags. Ben gave me my pink ball and then helped secure the latches. Mama barked at the front door and looked like she wanted to kill someone. I saw hatred in her eyes that I had never noticed before. She must have felt desperate watching us being loaded into Dumb Head's car. As much as I wished she could do something, I knew she was helpless.

As Dumb Head pushed the hatchback down, Mama's barks turned to cries. Her voice was muffled from within the house, but my sharp ears caught most of what she said. "Goodbye, my puppies! My beautiful children, I will always love you! Remember everything I taught you, and be good for your new owners! I love you!"

Hearing her words and cries made me whimper. I realized that it was real; that I would never see Mama again. Alice and Ben would be out of my life for good. What would I do without them? Where would I live? My siblings cried with me as we slowly pulled out of the driveway. Their whines were soft at first, but then escalated to high-pitched howling. We fed off of one another until I noticed that Dumb Head had covered his ears.

"Shut up, you dag-gone sissies!" he screeched from the front seat.

At the top of the driveway, Ben stood beside Alice and stared our way. Kicking dust into the air, we turned onto the road. I saw them get smaller and smaller until they were gone.

Chapter Three

Dumb Head

Buff Cooper was a man of few scruples. He didn't really care for other people, and the only dog he liked was his own. Although he had a lucrative business, Buff started dealing puppies after his last divorce and continued because it paid cash and his secretary did all the work. He had won custody of his ex-wife's male shepherd and, being the shrewd businessman that he was, figured he could stud the dog and make good money. Buff knew that people would pay a pretty penny for purebreds, as long as the dogs had show papers and a family lineage. He also knew that most people were gullible, especially when it came to cute little puppies. All Buff had to do was find stupid people and create believable documents. The rest was a piece of cake.

Alice, Ben, and their dog were a perfect match for Buff. When he met the simple couple through an ad in the paper, he felt like he had struck gold. Folks like that never asked questions, and they never broke their word. So when Buff drove away that day with five money-making mutts, he chuckled to himself for a job well done. He could already feel the cash in his wallet.

An Unnamed Dog

When we reached our destination, it seemed like the whole day had passed, even though the sun still hung high in the sky. Riding in the car had been stressful. With every turn, I slid from one side of the crate to the other, crashing into the metal bars and flopping onto my side. By the time we stopped, my skin hurt and my head was sore. I was glad to be somewhere.

As I looked through the windows, I saw tops of gray buildings and smokestacks. It seemed strange and bare. When Dumb Head opened the hatchback, there was more of the same. A whole new world had opened in front of me. It was ugly and empty, and I didn't like it.

The first thing I noticed was that the ground was black and hard with white lines painted in between the cars. The only green around was from a few skinny trees that grew sparsely alongside the blacktop. Grass sprouted in scattered brown patches, and there were wooden picnic tables that covered most of it. Trash lay strewn on the ground, blowing from one spot to another in the hot breeze. People in blue uniforms sat at the tables reading newspapers or eating sandwiches, while others unloaded boxes from a truck nearby and laughed loudly. Machinery hummed quietly off in the distance.

Dumb Head stood propped against the hatchback, holding his phone in one hand and looking around. He grunted and glanced at his watch several times, until a woman came running out of the nearest building and toward the car. When he saw her, he smiled and followed her with his eyes. She flitted past him with a happy nod of acknowledgment, then leaned inside the car and looked at us. Her face lit up, and she squealed and jiggled with excitement. She puckered her shiny pink lips and

widened her eyes so her thick lashes touched her brows.
"Ooh, look at the babies. Look at the little, precious babies.
Come here and see me. Ooh, come here." She unlatched the
crates and pulled us out one by one, letting us lick her lips. Her
arms splayed across the opening, exposing her buxom chest as
she leaned into us. I sniffed her ear, while some of my brothers
crawled down her shirt. The woman giggled and pulled them
out. She had long painted nails with sparkles on them.

I had forgotten about Dumb Head for the time being.
Not until he patted the woman from behind did I give him a
thought. She shrieked and bumped her head on the ceiling of
the car.

"Buff!" She smacked his hand away and frowned. Buff
must have been his other name.

Dumb Head chuckled and stuffed his hands into his
pockets. He puffed his chest out and leaned back against the
car with a weird smirk on his face. "Nice looking shepherds,
eh?"

"Oh, they're just precious," she replied, smiling once again
and fluffing our heads.

"Yeah, they're better looking than the last batch except for
this huge one here." He nodded and pointed at me. "Hopefully, someone doesn't mind his size, 'cause I'm not willing to
lose money on any of these dogs this time."

The nice woman purposely pulled me away from the rest
of the group while Dumb Head blocked the others' escape. She
stuck her nose into my neck while lifting me under the armpits
with her chubby hands. Her face wiggled back and forth in my
fur, and her breath smelled like fruit punch and chocolate.

"Ooh, I'll take this big, mushy guy. He's sooo cute, and I
love his big face." She looked into my eyes and squeezed me

against her chest. She was soft and cozy, and I liked her. "Come on Mr. Mush," she said. "Let's go inside where we can get you some water and goodies." She cradled me in her arms, and we walked toward the building.

"Hey, sweetheart, just stick him in the pen and come right back out. I'm not payin' you to slouch, Dora!" Dumb Head yelled, as the door shut behind us.

"Yeah, whatever, you jerk," Dora said, under her breath.

We entered a large concrete room and were greeted by a big male German shepherd.

"So, what do we have here?" asked the dog, as he sniffed under my tail.

"It's okay, big guy," she said to me. "That's just Big Daddy. He's Buff's dog, and he's very friendly." She continued to carry me toward the middle of the room.

"Just call me Big D, little infant, and don't think I'll be so nice just 'cause I donated the goods," the dog said, following behind us and checking me out. Then we stopped. "You're huge," he said, sounding pleased. "I guess my boys are doin' their job." Big D walked away, swinging his tail. I didn't understand anything he said.

Big D lumbered over to a big round bed in the corner. Other than him, the room was plain but nice. It was surprisingly cool and dry with a constant breeze. The lights were bright and made a humming noise. Across the way were two messy desks, surrounded by metal cabinets stacked with papers and books. At Dora's feet was a large gated pen that was about the size of Alice and Ben's laundry room. The fence was no higher than Dora's knees. She set me down gently.

"I'll be right back, big Mush."

Within a couple seconds, Dumb Head dumped two more

of us in the pen. Then Dora brought the last two. Five total. One more time, Big D got out of his bed and sniffed each of my siblings as they were set down. Just like he had done with me, he nodded his approval and went back to bed.

Dora dropped into the pen all the rags and toys that Alice had sent. Each of us had our favorite toy. My ball was the last thing in, and I was relieved. Dora had new toys for us too. There were some different kinds of balls, a stuffed Frisbee, some rawhide bones, and a few knotted socks. There were also newspapers on the floor and two large dog beds. The beds didn't look new, but they were clean and they smelled like Big D. Two bowls of water sat in the corner of the pen. The fence itself was wooden with criss-crosses. I liked it.

"Hey, Dora, did you get that ad in the paper?" Dumb Head watched her as she bent over to arrange the toys. She stepped over us like we were made of glass.

"Uh, hang on Buff," she used her finger to count, "one, two, three, four, five...uh, yeah." She looked down as she stepped over the gate. "Yes, I did it while you were picking them up. Here." She pulled a piece of folded paper out of her skirt pocket and handed it to him.

Dumb Head pushed his glasses against his face and read the message in a serious voice. "Purebred German shepherd puppies, kennel association approved, six weeks old, shots up to date, show-quality mother and champion stud, four hundred twenty-five dollars." He put the piece of paper on his desk and gave Dora an approving look. "Sounds good, honey." He gave her a wink and a nod.

Dora placed her hands on her hips and cocked her head. "Have they really had their shots, Buff?"

"Of course they have," he lied. Mama told us about shots,

but we hadn't gotten them yet.

"Okay, good. Well, at least this time they look like German shepherds." Dora giggled as she looked at us.

"They are German shepherds, Dora!" Buff shot back angrily.

Dora softened. "Oh, Buff, I'm just teasing. I know you didn't mean to breed Big Daddy to a stupid terrier last time." She rolled her eyes, then went over to where he stood and straightened his tie. His shoulders relaxed, and the redness faded from his face.

Buff sighed as he pulled away from her and sat down at his desk. "All I can say, darlin', is that you're darned lucky to have me as your boss." He slid off his shoes and put his feet up on a pile of papers, wiggling his toes. "I'm not sure anyone else would find you that funny—or cute for that matter. Here, rub my feet, sweetie." He leaned back and farted.

Dora had already started to walk away. She wrinkled her nose as she turned her face toward us. "I suppose you're right, Buff. I'm the luckiest secretary ever."

That first day pretty much set the tone for how things would be. Dumb Head didn't take any interest in us, except when he showed us to prospective buyers. Dora seemed to work overtime to be with us more often. Big Daddy slept all day and went home with Buff at night. His only daily words were, "Keep it down, please. My boys need their rest."

I loved Dora and relied on her the most. She fed us, gave

us fresh water, and took us outside to go potty. When she had extra time, she played with us. In the evenings before she left, she would turn on the TV so we had company throughout the long, dark night. Her presence was so comforting that all we really needed was to have her nearby. I was happy for the most part until my siblings began to go home with strangers. My sister was the first to go. Then the rest of them left, one by one, until it was just me.

Chapter Four

Trudy

The old lady sat in her armchair and stared at the wall. It was three o'clock in the morning, and she couldn't sleep. Not only had she suffered from insomnia lately, but she was worried that she hadn't locked the front door. At ten o'clock, when she had retired to her bedroom, she only remembered stopping in the kitchen for a glass of water. But, memory loss was a common nuisance lately, and leaving doors unlocked was just one of many things. If she could have mustered the energy, she would have checked the door hours ago. But being in the state that she was, it wasn't worth fracturing a hip. Besides, if an intruder happened to break into her house, it was probably God's way of punishing her.

Rather than fretting over events she couldn't control, the tired old woman relaxed in her chair and tried to reminisce about happier times. When she finally fell asleep, she was tormented by yet another nightmare that left her wondering why on earth she still lived.

An Unnamed Dog

I had another nightmare.

It was late at night. The air was chilly, and the moon was full. Leaves had just begun to form on the trees, whose branches dipped lazily in the thick spring air. A balmy breeze trickled past my nose, carrying the smell of fresh grass, new soil, and perfume from the rose garden.

I was aware of subtle noises on our farm that night. The chickens clucked innocently in their sleep. Water snakes and turtles rippled in the pond behind me, and field mice crunched and scurried over the stiff weeds. Bullfrogs croaked in continuous waves, and crickets hummed and buzzed in harmony. Every now and then, I heard horses from a distant farm whinny and buck at the threat of a predator. Patiently, I would ignore the cries, unless our chickens went into a sudden frenzy. Then it was my job to chase the unwelcome animal away.

I slept in a doghouse outside of my family's home. It was made of sturdy wood siding and a real shingled roof. A bed of thick straw kept me warm, and I had a full view of my house and the dirt road beyond. I was a watchdog, and my job was to protect my family.

That particular night, something more dangerous than an animal trespassed onto my property. I had just fallen asleep when I heard grass crunching somewhere between the house and the road. It came from footsteps that were heavy and human-like. I lifted my body ever so quietly and craned my neck around the doorway of my doghouse. Since it was dark and my views were limited, I took a step outside and paused to listen. This time I heard a click and a scrape. It was the same sound as my owner's key unlocking the door, but as though the wrong key were being used. My senses heightened, and my pulse quickened. I knew I had to go to the other side of the house in order to catch the predator. My whole family slept inside, and I was afraid that they were in danger.

The hair on my neck tingled, and a low growl escaped from deep inside my throat as I crept quietly toward the front yard. Slowly, I passed the side windows while hiding in the shadows of the moon. As I neared the door, I heard breathing. It was quick and nervous. Whenever the scraping noise resumed, the breathing paused and I could take another few steps. Just as I got to the front of the house, I peered around the corner and saw a tall figure in a black coat and mask. He stood by the door and looked around carefully. He then pushed the door inward and advanced into the house. A piece of metal in the shape of a knife reflected from his hand.

As he disappeared through the doorway, visions of my family ran through my mind. I knew if anything happened, it would be my fault. My entire body reacted as I broke into a ground-breaking lunge, kicking up massive amounts of dirt as my back feet dug into the ground. I charged the intruder at light-ning speed, barking ferociously and breaking through the door. Not completely inside the house yet, he turned toward me—the whites of his eyes glowing in the light of the moon. As I leaped at his throat, he dropped the metal object and fell backward, screaming wildly, "No, no, get off me! Get off me!" He kicked and struggled, ripping at my fur with such force that I could feel the burning pain of skin as it was pulled from my muscle. I bit more forcefully into his neck until I tasted his hot, metallic blood. As his screams turned to moans, I heard two female voices and the sounds of footsteps banging anxiously down the stairs. The porch light flipped on, exposing my intruder, and he finally stopped struggling. From the kitchen, I heard my owner dial the phone and repeat that she needed someone at her house immediately because there was a burglar. I stayed where I was and held onto the man, even though he had stopped moving. The other female who had come downstairs cried as my owner tried to calm her down.

"Julie, stop it!" she said in a loud whisper. "Thor's got the burglar by the neck. He's not going to hurt us. Go over to Mr. Jason's house, and tell him we need his help until the police get here. Tell him your father's out of town, and we need a man's help. Go, now. Hurry!"

Julie pulled her robe together and ran through the living room and out the side door. In the distance, the sound of a siren approached.

My beautiful owner was visibly shaken. I watched her as she gathered her courage, straightened her hair with both hands, and went to the cupboard, pulling a pistol from the top shelf. She walked over to where I stood and pointed the gun at my head. Her face was so lovely in the moonlight, and I thought she must have made a mistake. But she just looked at me as she started to cry and said, "I'm so sorry, Thor, my boy. I love you so much, and I don't want to kill you."

I panicked and began to choke on the intruder's blood. Backing away from the job I had been so proud of, I looked at my owner in disbelief. She was going to shoot me. My owner that loved me so much was going to kill me.

She cried louder and harder, until tears made of blood poured from her eyes. "Thor, I love you, but I have to kill you!"

Her hands shook as she held the gun, and her face melted like wax, dripping down the front of her nightgown. I turned my body to run, but I felt like I weighed a thousand pounds. I was stuck standing over the intruder who now twisted in pain. I had to drag myself with all my might to get off of him, and when I finally broke free, I woke up.

It took forever to realize I was okay. I still ran as my paws moved and twitched, and my chest heaved. I looked around to find nobody next to me, just my ball tucked snugly under my chest. The TV glowed from the far side of the room, while the fan blew cool air over my back. I had never felt so lonely and scared in all my life.

Chapter Five

An Unnamed Dog

That night I never went back to sleep. I stayed huddled in the corner of my pen and couldn't shake the lonely chill off my bones. I kept picturing the woman in my dream holding a gun to my head. Who was she? It was the second time I had dreamt of her. It was the same house, the same yard, and I was the same dog named Thor. I couldn't get rid of the feeling that I knew her, yet in my short life I hadn't met anyone who fit her description. I certainly couldn't think of anyone who wanted to kill me.

Suddenly, I jumped at the sound of Dora's key engaging the big steel door. She walked into the warehouse smiling.

"Good morning, my special mushy puppy. I am soooooo happy to see you."

She came over to me before she had a chance to take off her sweater. Setting her purse down on the floor, she scooped me into her big soft arms. "Ooh, you're getting so heavy." She nestled her fresh-smelling face into the side of my neck and gave me a bunch of short kisses. Then she held me up and looked straight at me, her nose almost touching mine. "How was your night last night, Mister? I bet you were so lonely." She cradled me back into her arms and, as she talked, flipped off the TV and pulled open a blind. "I asked Buff if I could take you home with me last night, but he wouldn't let me. He said it would confuse you too much. Your first night without your brothers must have been really hard on you." She was right about that. I wished I'd gone home with her.

She took me outside. While I walked and sniffed, she continued to talk. "Well, I have some good news for you, big boy. Buff talked to a family yesterday, and they're interested in meeting you. I think they're coming over this afternoon." Then her voice changed. "The only thing I'm worried about is that the man is a policeman. I was married to one a couple years ago, and the only thing he thought dogs were good for was to guard the house and scare people away. He wasn't very loving." Her voice turned sweet again. "We had this German shepherd that looked just like you, Mushy. My ex-husband didn't like him because Bruno was afraid of thunder. That dirt bag would purposely shoot his gun around Bruno just to scare him. I finally left his sorry butt." She shook her head and looked down. "God bless my Bruno, he was such a sweetheart. He died of old age shortly after the divorce, and I still miss him." Her eyes came back to me. "But anyway, my ex wasn't a nice guy. That doesn't mean they're all like that, of course. I adored his coworkers. I should have married one of them." She hesitated while I watered a tiny flower. "All that matters is that someone loves you as much as I do. I would take you home if I could."

As we headed back to our building, I let Dora's words settle and realized I might actually have a family. I might go home with someone forever, just like my brothers and sister. Even though I loved Dora, I felt excited. I watched cop shows at night, and police officers were always heroes. They saved nice guys from bad guys and rescued dogs from terrible homes. My policeman would for sure be wonderful. He would be handsome in his uniform, with a wife that was just like Dora.

They would have two happy children that played baseball and took me for walks. The family would drive a big car and, most importantly, have a home in the country where I could run and chase deer.

When we got back to the warehouse, we were greeted by Big D who, seeing it was only us, went back to bed. Dumb Head sat at his desk eating a cinnamon roll that dripped white frosting down his tie. Dora made the mistake of looking at the bun. Dumb Head immediately shook his finger at her while he quickly swallowed his food.

"Uh uh, sweetheart, you don't need the calories. Stop drooling like the dogs," he scolded, spewing crumbs into the air. Dora stood silent, then shook her head and walked away. I wanted to pee in his shoe but was placed back in my pen where I quietly chewed a sock.

"I've got some stuff for you to do here, honey, and then the copper and his wife are coming to look at the mutt." Dumb Head wiped his fat lips with the back of his hand; then he stood up and stretched. As his arms moved upward, his shirt came out of his belt, and a hairy wad of fat popped out from under the buttons. His armpits were soaked with yellow sweat, and he had brown dough stuck in his teeth. With a disgusted look on her face, Dora turned and followed Dumb Head obediently out the door.

Nearing lunchtime, I took my usual nap. Dora yacked on the phone, and Dumb Head read something on his computer, looking at his watch every now and then. As it got later, he fidgeted more, drumming his fingers on his desk and tapping his feet. Suddenly the doorbell buzzed. Dumb Head stood up and checked himself in a mirror. He brushed some hair off his pants and straightened his tie. After peering through the tiny hole in the door, he opened it.

So many things ran through my mind at that moment. I thought about Dora's ex-husband and how he treated his dog. I also thought about my perfect family and wondered what their house would be like. I wondered about the kids who would live there and how they would act. Then, I thought back to Alice and Ben and felt momentarily homesick. My stomach twisted in knots as I waited to see who would walk through the door. Maybe they wouldn't want me, and I could relax again. Or, maybe I shouldn't think about it and let things happen. Unfortunately, I was just a dog and had already learned that I didn't have a choice either way. My future was entirely up to Dumb Head.

When the family walked into the warehouse, I think we were all surprised.

"Come in, come in," Dumb Head said with a big fake smile as he ushered his guests through the entrance with a swoop of his hand. "You must be the lovely Melon family."

"It's Meloon," corrected the man, stressing the "oo," like "balloon." He walked through the door followed by his pregnant wife and two young children. It was obvious he didn't appreciate being called a fruit.

As I studied the family, I felt neither excited nor afraid. Mr. Meloon didn't fit my picture of the handsome policeman at all. Instead, he was a nerdier version of Dumb Head, if that was possible. He had the lanky body of a teenage boy, stood as tall as Dora, and had a narrow face with protruding cheek bones and crooked teeth. His skin was pitted with scars, and his blond greasy hair receded back on his narrow forehead. The pants he wore were tight against his legs and fastened high above his waist. His shirt was unbuttoned and showed a hairless chest. When he talked, his voice squeaked as he looked at the floor. He didn't seem happy or fun, and my feelings about him weren't good.

Mrs. Meloon, on the other hand, looked nice but didn't say anything. She nodded when her husband talked and tried to keep a hand on her smallest son's shoulder. She was gentle with her children and dressed in a plain smock that wore thin around her pregnant middle. Her shoes were frumpy but clean, and her face was plain and pale.

The children were perfect. The minute they saw me, their eyes widened and they looked like they would burst from excitement. But, rather than running and screaming across the room like other kids I had met, they first went up to their dad. The bigger one tapped on his arm.

"Dad, can we go over and see the puppy, please?"

"Boys, remember your manners and shake Mr. Cooper's hand," Mr. Meloon said sternly. He placed his hands on each of their heads and turned their faces toward Buff.

"Nice to meet you, sir," they said in unison, looking at the ground as they shook his hand.

"Now can we go?" asked the smaller one this time.

"Yes, and be careful. Puppies bite." Mr. Meloon released his grip on their heads, and they ran over to me.

I was thrilled. I stood with my paws on the gate and barked. My tail wagged and my butt wiggled. The boys climbed into my pen, and I jumped on them, knocking them over. Mrs.

Meloon stared nervously as they giggled and rolled on the ground, letting me grab their shoelaces. She must have thought they were too rough with me, but she didn't say a word and was ignored by Mr. Meloon. She stood biting her nails as her husband chatted with Dumb Head.

Finally there was a break in the adult conversation. We sat sweaty and tired from playing so hard, and Mr. Meloon looked over at us.

"So Dad, are we going to buy him? Pleeeaaase, can we buy him?" the older boy asked, out of breath. With one hand he petted my back, and with the other he tossed my ball up and down.

Mr. Meloon was about to respond when the younger boy interrupted. "Yeah, Dad, please can we get him? Please, please, Dad, please?" He got out of the pen and began to jump up and down, twirling and clapping.

The older one stood up and paused for a moment, staring at his mother. When she smiled, he began to jump also. He placed my ball in his shirt pocket and sang in unison with his brother. They sounded like cheerleaders. "Please, Dad, please! Please, Dad, please!"

I watched Mr. Meloon narrow his eyebrows. His face turned red and angry, and his fists clenched down by his thighs. Mrs. Meloon's mouth closed the minute she saw his face. She looked nervously to the boys, but it was too late. Mr. Meloon lost his temper. "Stop it, boys! Enough, already! I will not have you jumping around like a couple of idiots in public!"

The boys instantly froze and hung their heads in shame. The younger one's lip began to quiver. Dora looked from Mr. Meloon to me. I could see the disappointment in her face and knew what she must have thought. As tears welled in her eyes, she excused herself from the room.

Mr. Meloon didn't take his eyes off of the boys. "Now act like you have brains, and take yourselves out to the truck before you embarrass me anymore. Your mother and I will come out with the dog in just a minute."

The boys followed his instructions and left the warehouse. The door shut behind them, and I realized that this was the family I was going home with. This was my new family. The Meloon family. But Mr. and Mrs. Meloon hadn't even met me yet. They hadn't seen me up close or petted my fur. How did they know they would like me? Maybe they just wanted me for the kids. That was fine. I liked the kids and wanted to sleep in their rooms anyway. The more I imagined my new life, the more excited I became and wanted desperately to get out to the car. I stood with my paws on the gate and barked.

Mr. Meloon didn't budge, and Mrs. Meloon's eyes didn't leave the door that her boys had just exited. She began to bite her nails again.

"Stop doing that," Mr. Meloon said crossly to his wife.

Mrs. Meloon stopped.

"Well then, Mr. Meloon," Dumb Head over-pronounced the "oo." "There's your big, scary police dog. He's a smart one, and he scares the heck out of my secretary, which is probably why she left," he lied. "Although he's hardly old enough to hurt anyone right now, I'm sure you can train him well."

Mr. Meloon smiled for the first time and turned his gaze in my direction. "Oh, I don't think I want him to hurt anyone. I just want the proper protection for my family." He walked toward me and took his wife by the arm. "Come on, Marion, don't be such a chicken." He pulled her, and she reluctantly followed. "Let's go see the dog I just paid a week's wages for."

Running Home

"All right, Jim," she replied.

Dumb Head stood behind them, rolling his eyes.

As Jim and Marion Meloon approached me, I put my best face on and wagged my tail harder than ever. Jim squatted in front of me, and Marion peered over his shoulder. Neither one of them said anything. There were no "oohs" or "ahhs." They didn't even smile.

Dumb Head chuckled and strolled over, shaking his head and rubbing his chin. "Here folks, all you do is pick 'im up like so, and he'll know right away who's boss." He grabbed me by the scruff of my neck and lifted me to Jim's face. I cried because it hurt, and Marion shrieked.

Jim quickly took me out of Dumb Head's grasp. Holding me out in front of him, he said, "It's okay, I got him. I know how to handle these dogs." His voice was arrogant, but his hand trembled as he held me. I was just glad to be away from Dumb Head.

Jim put me back on the ground and took a leash from his pocket. I wanted him to pet my head and say hello, but he never did. I could tell he was frustrated trying to attach the leash to my collar as he struggled to keep me still. Beads of sweat formed on his forehead while his fingers fiddled and slipped on the clasp. Finally he got it and stood up.

"Okay, let's go," he said as I pulled at the leash. He followed me, and Marion followed him. Right before we got to the door, I stopped. There was one more thing I wanted to do before I said goodbye. I wanted to pee in Dumb Head's shoes. Heading in the direction of his desk, I angled past his extra pair of "favorite" shoes and lifted my leg. I watered them until they were good and soaked, and by the time Dumb Head saw what I did, I was done.

34

Chapter Five

"Hey, you little creep!" Dumb Head ran toward me, but I hustled quickly behind Jim's legs.

As we walked out the door, I never looked back.

Chapter Six

An Unnamed Dog

When we got to the parking lot, I searched for a truck. I wanted a big one that had plenty of room in the back. If not, I was sure the boys wouldn't mind sharing their seat with me.

We walked past tons of cars, a few motorcycles, and some delivery trucks. I saw Dora's favorite picnic table, my preferred fire hydrant, and the dumpster that smelled bad. I looked and looked for that big wonderful truck that I pictured so vividly, but couldn't find it. As Jim led Marion and me across the hot asphalt, I heard the voices of the boys and turned my head in their direction. All I saw, parked alone next to the dumpster, was a small black pickup with a metal crate sitting in the bed. The truck looked barely big enough for a family of four, let alone one that had a dog. As we stopped at the tailgate, two smiling faces and four waving hands thrust out the back window.

"Yay, it's the dog! Yay!" The boys looked like they would pop out of the small opening. The younger boy's hands pounded the top of the crate that was tied on with a rope.

"Get back in your seats!" Jim yelled. "Steven, stop banging on the cage! Tommy, shut the window!"

I was suddenly terrified. I realized that the crate was there for me. As Jim lifted me over the side of the truck, I began to fight. I wanted to ride with the boys and couldn't understand why I had to be alone outside. There had to be room for me on someone's lap, and if not, the floor would have been fine. But Jim was persistent. He forced me through the door of the crate, then latched it tight. I saw the boys lock the back window while Jim got in the driver's seat. As the engine revved and smoke blew out of the back of the truck, my new family and I drove away from the warehouse.

We continued for some time on the road, my crate rattling and shaking the entire time. I was deaf in the open air, and just like in Dumb Head's car, I slid around and slammed into the metal bars with every turn. When we finally got off the highway and headed in a different direction, the setting changed. The road became wider with more stoplights. Giant tractor-trailers crowded the lanes and burped black smoke and heavy fumes. The air was hazy and speckled with exhaust that billowed from the tops of buildings. Most everything looked old and worn. The storefronts were dirty with crumbling bricks and crooked street numbers. Restaurants I had seen advertised on TV flashed brightly colored signs. As we passed them, I recognized the wonderful smell of hamburgers and french fries that Dumb Head ate everyday at his desk.

Before I knew it, we turned into a tree-lined neighborhood with hundreds of houses set in perfect rows. Each house was identical to the one before it, except for its color. Every backyard was fenced with a long driveway that led to a small garage. No farther than five houses from the busy road, Jim pulled into one of the driveways. He stopped short of the gate and turned off the truck's sputtering engine.

"We're home!" yelled the boys from the back seat.

I felt pity for the Meloon family as I looked at our pathetic house. It was a tiny, vomit-colored, two-story structure that sat on a cracked driveway and small yard. What grass there was looked freshly cut and well maintained, but the house's garage was an eyesore. Pieces of the siding were missing, and the roof sagged with green moss. The garage door was broken and hung crooked as if it was about to fall off.

The only thing I liked about the outside of my new home was the two large maple trees that stood so tall and wide. They covered the whole backyard and most of the roof. I knew I would love the inside of the house too, especially the boys' bedrooms. I already decided that's where I would spend most of my day, lying among stuffed animals, balls, and dirty shoes. Then at night, we would curl up in bed like clumps of puppies and sleep soundly.

As I waited for someone to let me out of the crate, I noticed my reflection in the window of the truck. Dora called me mushy because my nose was flatter and I had longer hair when we first met. But in just the time I had lived at the warehouse, my nose had gotten longer and my hair was shorter around my ears. The coloring on my face was still mostly black, but I had started to form the mask of an adult German shepherd. My paws were huge, and I thought I looked a little chubby. But I didn't care. I loved to eat and was hungry all the time.

The family piled out of the truck, and the boys ran around to let me out. Jim stopped them just as they were about to climb onto the tailgate.

"Boys, no! I don't want you letting the dog into the street. I'm the only one allowed to handle him while we're in the front yard, do you understand?"

The boys froze and looked at their dad with a fast nod and a giggle. They began to jump up and down again. Jim shook his head in disgust and leaned over to open the crate. He picked me up gently, and said, "Okay, dog, this is your new home. Don't destroy it."

He carried me inside the open gate and set me on the pavement. The boys and Marion followed behind. Marion waddled into the house, while the kids rushed to my side. They walked with me as I sniffed out my new yard.

Jim brushed his hands together and then folded his arms. "All right, boys, be careful with the dog and don't roughhouse too much. He's got a job here like everyone else, and I don't want him spoiled with constant play. You have a few minutes to show him around the yard, and then your mother will call you in for lunch."

I could already hear dishes clanking from inside the house and saw Marion's face peering out of the open kitchen window. "Tommy and Steven, be careful, and don't give that dog any reason to bite you."

"Yes, Mother."

While Jim took the crate out of the truck and stuck it under the garage door, Tommy walked behind one of the trees and pulled my pink ball out from under his sweatshirt. "Look, boy, I brought the ball with us since we don't have any here."

I was so happy to see my ball and was even happier when Tommy threw it to the back of the yard. Steven ran with me to fetch it and then we rolled on the freshly cut grass. He giggled, and I barked. Tommy joined us after a few seconds, realizing I wasn't bringing the ball back.

"Come on, let's play hide and seek!" yelled Tommy.

"Steven, count to twenty!" I followed Tommy as he ran around to the front of the garage and then under the broken door. We stopped in the middle of the dark, dank structure, and I noticed my crate had been placed in the corner. It took a few moments before my eyes adjusted to the blackness. Stacked against the wall were old chairs, rusty rakes, and a lawn mower. The floor was half concrete and half dirt, and cobwebs stretched from rafter to rafter. It was scary because the only light that came in was through the broken door, the holes in the siding, and two dirty windows.

"Come on, boys, it's time for lunch!" Marion called.

Tommy and I ran out to the driveway. Marion stood at the side door, holding it open. As Steven ran past us and into the house, Tommy and I followed. As soon as I was about to enter, someone grabbed me from behind.

"No, dog! Not you. You stay outside where you belong." Jim threw me back onto the concrete and followed Marion through the doorway. As the screen door shut behind him, he looked back at me. "Bad dog!"

I sat there, confused and lonely. I cried as loud as I could and stood up against the door to see my family through the screen. Steven and Tommy ate at a table talking quietly to each other. Jim and Marion were silent.

"Dad, why can't he come in the house?"

Jim was stern. "Dogs don't belong inside the house, especially this kind of dog. He's here to protect our home, so no one breaks in. Like I told you earlier, he's a dog, not a toy, and I want him to know his place."

What did he mean dogs didn't belong inside the house? Where was I supposed to sleep, eat, and stay warm on cold nights? Who was going to be with me when I was lonely or sad? What was I going to do when I was bored and needed someone to play with? I couldn't believe what I heard. It was worse than my worst nightmare. I wondered if Dora would rescue me, or if Alice and Ben would find me and take me back to the farm. The day didn't seem real anymore as I sat outside and realized I would never go inside my own home.

When the boys came back out after lunch, they walked me to the small grassy area behind the garage.

"I'm sorry, boy," said Tommy sadly. "I didn't know you were gonna have to live in the garage all by yourself."

My stomach suddenly flipped, and I felt sick. I had to live in the garage?

"Yeah, puppy, we want you to live with us, but Dad said dogs like you can't live in a house," repeated Steven. "And, Mom is afraid of you and said you can't be around the new baby when it's born." He shook his head and sighed, "Stupid baby."

Tommy petted my back as I tried to chew his sleeve. "I promise we'll spend as much time as we can with you out here. We'll come out first thing in the morning and stay with you until late at night."

"Yeah, maybe we can even sleep in the garage with you!" said Steven. "We'll just tell Dad, 'Too bad.'"

But I had a feeling none of those things would happen.

The boys played with me for the rest of the afternoon, which kept my mind off of the obvious—nighttime alone in the garage. Jim only came out when he brought me a bowl of water.

"Here's some water, dog. Sit in the shade if it gets too hot, and there's a nice bed in the garage for you to sleep in. Most dogs would die to have what you have. I'll bring your dinner out at six." He placed the bowl on the driveway. As he turned to go back into the house, I jumped on his legs to get his attention. But he only spun around and shouted, "No! No jumping!"

Shortly before dinner, Marion called the kids in to wash up. Jim came outside with the food he had promised and took it inside the garage. I was too depressed to eat and wasn't interested in going back into that dark hole unless I had to. There was no TV to keep me company, no air conditioner to keep me cool, and no blanket in the crate. It was a dirty, dark, lonely place, and Jim thought I was lucky to have it.

As I sat outside the kitchen door and listened to the clink of silverware and quiet conversation, I thought about where I was for the first time that day. My new home wasn't anything like what I dreamed. It wasn't in the country. I didn't have a big yard or a nice house. My owner wasn't a handsome hero married to a woman like Dora. And, I would never play in a child's bedroom. Only a few crickets could be heard in my neighborhood, and I doubted I would ever chase a deer or even a squirrel. When I looked into the sky, I saw gray smog and clouds, rather than blue sky and sunshine. The sounds of factory machines and endless traffic were constant reminders of a nearby city.

The boys only came out one more time that night. Tommy carried a blue blanket into the garage, gave me a kiss on my nose, and said goodnight. Steven put his arms around me and told me he'd see me in the morning. From an upstairs window, I heard water running, followed later by the boys' laughing and splashing. Jim's voice was muffled in another part of the house and sounded like he was on the phone. I never heard Marion, but that seemed typical.

As the evening sky darkened, I walked to the back corner of the yard and went potty. I followed the fence around the entire perimeter, sniffing new smells and studying things that I hadn't seen yet. Back in the driveway, I drank from the bowl of water. It was warm, with dirt on the bottom and dead bugs floating on top. As I looked to the stars and saw none, I wondered why I was here, and if I'd ever be happy.

Chapter Seven

Clare

From up in the heavens, a man looked down on the puppy. He was disturbed to see where the dog had ended up. Not that he was particularly fond of dogs. But this dog was special. Someone he loved very much had asked for help, and he didn't want to let her down.

Ever since the man had died, he felt helpless. On Earth, he had been under the impression that his family was happy and his wife was content. But now that he was in heaven, he could hear people's thoughts and feel their pain. He knew his wife struggled with old events in her life that she couldn't control. Months ago, he listened to her as she pleaded with God for help. He was glad to see that the first part of her prayer had been answered. The dog had been reborn, and for that he was thankful. But the second part was still in question. The dog wasn't happy, which made the man feel guilty and responsible. He had let his wife down in the past and wanted to make things right, before he saw her again. So he made a decision. If there was a way he could guide the dog to a better life, he would try his best.

45

An Unnamed Dog

That first night in the garage was a true test of my courage. I had remained outside on the driveway for what seemed like forever, staring at the house and hoping for someone to let me in. I cried, whimpered, and jumped on the door, but it only made things worse. Jim turned on a loud fan and turned off the porch light. Although the distant sounds of nonstop traffic filled my ears, I felt like I was the only creature alive besides the moths that buzzed under the street lights.

What finally made me go into the garage was the rain. Clouds that had moped sluggishly all day slowly emptied their contents on our house. Reluctantly, I crept into my dark home and felt for the crate. It was still in the corner, and Tommy had put his blanket on the hard bottom along with my ball. I also remembered that Jim had put my food bowl somewhere in there, but I didn't see it. What I wanted most was company.

I soon found out that company wasn't hard to find in the Meloon's garage. It may not have been the kind I wanted, but at least I wasn't alone. Late in the night after the rain calmed and the traffic noises died to a lull, I began hearing something close to my crate. I wasn't sure if it had been there all night, but now it was obvious. It crunched, scuffled, and scratched just a shovel's length from where I lay. My first instinct was to pick up my ears and turn toward it. When it didn't stop, I growled and prepared to stalk. I felt my hair stand on end as I crept toward the noise. Wafts of dog food grew stronger with each step, which made me think that someone was feasting on my dinner. Not that I necessarily wanted to eat, but I suddenly felt the need to protect my bowl.

As I closed in on the noise, I made out several shadows

that moved along the floor. I didn't recognize the shapes, but I had heard about rats on TV commercials and figured that's what these were. They were pesky, disease-riddled, infection-causing rodents that required extermination from the professionals at "Rats 'R' Pus." But since I couldn't call the exterminator, I figured I'd handle the job myself.

When I was ready to pounce, I thought back to what Mama had taught me about hunting. "Never let them hear you coming," she used to say. "Even animals with eyes in the backs of their heads will miss you as long as you make yourself silent." So, as quietly as possible, I hunkered down and hooked my nails into the dirt floor. When the time was right, I lunged into the air, coming down paws-first in a forward slide. As I landed, the critters scattered like marbles, kicking up hundreds of kibbles as they shot in different directions. I scrambled to catch one, but only succeeded in spilling the rest of my food and banging into a broom which fell over and hit me in the back.

Exhausted, hungry, and sore from my act of bravery, I ate what was left of the kibbles and went back into my crate. I circled several times until I found a good spot. Then I curled up on Tommy's blanket and fell fast asleep. The only other thing I heard that night was a man's voice.

"Be patient, and I'll find you happiness," it said. I dreamt it just before I woke up to the sun peeking under the door. My head buzzed for a moment, but I chalked it off to a long night and a lot of stress. At least nobody tried to kill me. Today would have to be better.

Chapter Eight

Jim

Jim Meloon wasn't a happy man. Although he loved his family, he had a difficult time showing it. Friendships never came easy, either. In fact, there were only two people that Jim got along with. One was his wife. Another was his closest friend and partner, Officer Byron Anderson.

Jim met Byron several years before at the police academy, during a training exercise. While the two men worked out, Jim nearly fainted from heat exhaustion. Byron took him to the hospital, and they had remained friends ever since.

As planned, they hired on at the same police department and took their jobs very seriously. Their careers were like marriages to them and were thought of as life-long commitments. Both men had so much respect for the law that they tolerated little silliness from their colleagues. Neither was flexible or patient. Both had written up dozens of fellow officers in an attempt to correct their peers' ineptness and stupidity. Fortunately, the two men had each other to lean on. If not, they would have been forced to work with substandard idiots.

After ten years of service in the department, Jim and Byron thought they had it made. They were loyal husbands, strict fathers, and had pensions that would carry them to their deaths. But one night in late August, Jim's outlook changed drastically. While carrying out his normal day, he and Byron pulled a black sports car over for speeding. As Byron walked to the perpetrator's window for routine questioning, the driver took out a rifle and shot Byron dead.

An Unnamed Dog

I had lived with the Meloons long enough to figure out their daily habits. I also knew from conversations around the house that school would be starting soon, and Marion would have her baby. As I grew larger, so did her belly. Even though I could tell Jim was nervous about the upcoming birth, the day-to-day events never changed.

Every morning as the sun came up, Jim emerged from the house in his blue uniform. He would say good morning, put food in my bowl, and refill my water from the garden hose. In the kitchen, Marion would clank dishes and hum to the radio. Later on, the boys giggled cheerfully as they ate at the table and then crashed out of the side door with wet hands and milk mustaches. We would play most of the day until Jim got home.

Jim always arrived home as the sun sank behind the chimney. When his truck pulled up, I would stand with my paws on the gate until it swung open and he walked through. After receiving a swift knee in the gut for jumping, I would watch him walk into the house.

Jim faithfully brought my dinner out every night. After eating alone in the garage, I would lie by the side door while my family ate inside. It was always quiet at that time, but I loved it because my whole family was together. Unlike breakfast, there was no giggling or humming. Jim spoke every once in a while. He would tell the boys to chew with their mouths shut, or remind Marion that he didn't want to discuss this or that. I would relax in the driveway while smells of cooked meat and baked goods wafted through the kitchen window and into my nose.

After dinner, I would look through our fence as the dogs in our neighborhood took walks with their owners. I would get envious, but then the boys would run out and hug me goodnight. For a while, I felt loved and contented until the house turned dark and another lonely night took over.

"Good morning, puppy! How was your night? Did you sleep okay?" The boys raced out of the house and met me in the driveway. It was a beautiful morning that day, and they were already dressed. "Hey puppy, let's play with your ball! Go get your ball, good boy!"

I ran under the garage door and reemerged with my pink ball. The boys threw it for me until their arms were sore, and we all collapsed from exhaustion and heat. We lay sprawled out under the tree chewing on blades of grass while Tommy and Steven talked about what color backpacks they wanted for school. They also complained about their unborn brother or sister and tried to decide on a name for it.

"If it's a boy, we're going to name it Nicholas," said Steven.

"No we're not, Stevie," retorted Tommy. "Dad said the name would be Andrew."

"I like Nicholas." Steven scattered a handful of grass over my paws and looked at me with his head cocked. "I wish we had a name for you, puppy. Dad said it has to feel right, and he hasn't thought of one yet. He said he doesn't want to name you something stupid."

"Yeah, we have to name you something really cool like Spike or Killer," said Tommy with a smile.

"Mom hates those names, Tommy. They scare her."

"Whatever," sighed Tommy.

"I think we should name you Chocolate," said Steven.

"That's retarded," said his brother, "but what else would you expect from a kindergartener?"

"Yeah, well, you're a dumb second grader, and I hate you!" Steven stood up and threw a handful of grass at Tommy. He stomped toward the house, crying.

"Third grader!" Tommy yelled, correcting his brother. "He's such a baby." He turned back to me, shaking his head.

Marion ran out of the house. "What's wrong? Did the dog bite you, Steven?" She looked worried.

"No, I just hate Tommy." Steven walked past Marion into the house. She stood there for a while, staring at Tommy and me lying on the grass. Tommy ignored her until she went back inside.

"Mom worries too much. She always thinks you're going to bite us because she got bit by a dog when she was a kid. It's stupid."

After a while, he got up and brushed off his legs.

"I guess I'm gonna go to my friend Devin's house. See you later, boy. I'll be back at lunchtime." Tommy gave me another hug and walked off, leaving me alone under the tree. The air was heating up, and I figured I'd spend the remainder of the afternoon in my crate anyway.

When the sun went over the chimney that evening, Jim didn't come home. Marion was on the phone all afternoon, and the kids hadn't been back to the house until just before dinner. Nobody fed me that night, and nobody came outside. For whatever reason, things didn't go the way they were supposed to.

I stayed by the fence, watching dog after dog walk by, as the sun set lower in the sky. My stomach growled and whining by the door didn't help. Through the upstairs windows, the boys played loudly in their rooms, and I heard a TV from somewhere in the house.

Finally, long after dark, Jim's truck pulled into the driveway. I was relieved, but at the same time, Jim didn't look well. The moment he stepped out of the driver's door, he stumbled and almost fell. Marion's face appeared in the doorway, watching him silently, and I started to bark.

Jim looked up, and the porch light caught his face. His eyes and nose were red and swollen. His hair was out of place, and his uniform shirt was wet and rumpled. He turned and looked into my eyes for the first time ever. Then he started to cry. Not only did he cry, he sobbed. Tears poured out of his eyes like I'd never seen.

As he walked through the gate, he held on with both hands. He forgot to close his truck door, and papers scattered all over the pavement. Fiddling with the gate latch, his left hand came low enough where I could lick it. He surprisingly didn't push me away. I also smelled something sweet and pungent on his breath as he stumbled toward the house. His words slurred together, and I realized there was something terribly wrong with Jim.

"Oh, dog. Oh, my dog." Jim collapsed into a heap on the driveway and buried his face in his hands. His whole body shuddered as he moaned out loud, "Oh, God, help me. Why, God, why? Why did you have to take him? Why couldn't you take me?"

Take who? What was he saying? I noticed that the boys had joined Marion in the doorway. They all stared in disbelief.

Jim allowed me to climb onto his lap and lick his face as his body rocked back and forth in anguish. I wasn't sure if he even knew I was there; he was in such a state. But it didn't matter. It felt good to me. He put one hand on my back and left it there, while the other hand wiped his nose and rubbed his eyes. Then he took my whole body and hugged me.

"What am I going to do, dog? Who am I going to talk to? Oh, God, what am I going to do?"

When Tommy saw Jim holding me, I think he assumed he could comfort his father also. But when he stepped out of the door, Jim lost it.

"What are you doing out here! Get back in the house, boy! Get away from me! Marion, get those kids to bed!" He yelled so loud, I cowered as Marion and the kids retreated from the doorway. I tried to back off his lap, but he held me tighter. "No it's okay, not you. I don't care if you see me like this. You're just a dog." He sniffled and wiped his nose with his shirt. "But you're a smart dog, and you don't give me grief." Jim sat for a moment staring thoughtfully at the ground. Then his tone brightened. "Hey, how would you like the name of my best friend? I've been racking my brain for a while, and there's no better name than the name of a hero." He looked at me without diverting his gaze. His eyes were all red. "Byron. Yeah. Byron." And with that, Jim turned the other way and threw up all over the driveway.

Byron? My name was Byron. I had never heard it, I wasn't sure that I liked it, but it was good that I had a name. Or, was it? Because from that night on—the night I got my name—the Meloon family was never the same again.

Chapter Nine

Byron

The weeks following Officer Byron's death and my name-giving marked a drastic change in my life. Marion had her baby, the boys went back to school, and Jim stopped coming home after work. He must have forgotten our recent bonding experience because he returned to ignoring me the next day. In fact, he almost looked at me with contempt.

One of the last times I saw Jim interact with his whole family together was the day Marion had her baby. It was late morning, and I heard Tommy on the phone frantically trying to locate his dad.

"Could you please tell my dad, Officer Jim Meloon, that my mom's going to have her baby... No, it's Meloooon, Jim Meloon... Yes, she's having a baby and she needs him to come home right now." He paused again. "No, a baby! Just tell him that my mom has to go to the hospital!" Tommy pleaded.

Minutes later, Jim's patrol car screeched to a halt in front of the house.

"What's wrong?" Jim ran up the driveway. Marion and the boys waited for him just inside the door.

"Mom's gonna have her baby," Tommy said in a panicked voice.

"Is that the emergency that dispatch pulled me away for? Which one of you called 911?" Jim's face got red, and he looked angry. "Of all people, did my own wife have to make it sound like someone's dying, for God's sake! Go get your bags, Marion. Let's go." Jim yelled so loud that a neighbor across the street stopped what she was doing and stared.

Marion waddled out of the door, her hand over her belly and tears running down her cheeks. Tommy and Steven hurried behind her and got into the back seat of the patrol car while Jim plunked down in the driver's seat and pulled away. I sat for the remainder of the day and night patiently awaiting their return. They didn't get back until the following evening.

Three days after Baby Andrew came home, Tommy and Steven returned to school with the same backpacks they wore last year. Neither was happy about that or their new brother. Besides, their father hadn't kept his promise of walking them to class on their first day.

"But Mom, I don't want to go to school by myself. I don't know where my room is, and Steven doesn't even know who his teacher is," Tommy cried. "Please, can't you call Dad and ask him to come home and take us?" He was in tears as Marion stood with both boys on the front porch in her bathrobe, holding the crying newborn. She placed one hand on Tommy's shoulder.

"Tommy, you know how your dad's been lately. He's had too much stress in his life to remember school," said Marion gently.

Tommy pushed her hand away and stomped off the porch, grabbing Steven as he went. Marion stood helplessly watching them as they walked down the block. I knew she hadn't slept because of the dark circles under her eyes and the way her face was swollen. Besides, I had become familiar with the endless glow of her bedroom light and the noise of the crying infant all night long.

That type of day became normal for our family. Jim rarely came home, Marion looked more helpless than ever, and Steven threw constant temper tantrums. The only family member who still paid attention to me was Tommy. As unhappy as he looked, he hugged me in the morning and before he went to bed. If he noticed that my water was gone or my food bowl was empty, he filled them. But the things we used to enjoy together, like playing ball or lying under the tree, rarely happened. By the time dinner was over in the evenings, the sky was already dark and he wasn't allowed outside. I was lonelier than ever.

Jim's behavior had also become weird. Most of the time he ignored me. But when he came home in his bizarre state of mind, smelling sweet and talking nonsense, he liked me. He would call me by my name and tell me how he was going to train me. At those times, I felt proud and wanted to please him. But by the next morning, it was the same old thing.

One evening when the air was cool and the sky was dark, I thought Jim would finally take me for a walk. The trees were almost bare, and there was a refreshing wind that made the fallen leaves swirl on the driveway. Jim hadn't worked that day, and he and Marion had just finished arguing. She accused him of not taking care of his responsibilities anymore. It was the first time I had ever heard her yell at Jim.

"At least get rid of the dog!" she screamed from inside the kitchen. "It sits outside all day pacing back and forth, and it looks scary and mangy. You don't take care of it, half the time you forget to feed it, and the boys are too young to have that kind of responsibility. They can't even play outside anymore, Jim. The dog has ruined the grass, and there's poop everywhere!"

Rather than fighting back, Jim stormed out of the house

holding my leash. I didn't care that he was mad. I was just excited to go somewhere. I jumped on his legs and bit at the leash.

"Okay, okay, settle down so I can get this thing on you." Just like that first day, he attempted to attach the clasp to my collar. "Stop moving, Byron!" The scars on his face turned purple, and I knew he was about to lose it.

With all my jumping, biting, and wiggling, Jim gave up. He threw the leash onto the driveway and stomped back inside the house. I heard him take the keys out of his jacket and fumble for his wallet, all the while mumbling, "What's the use. Stupid family, stupid dog, stupid house, stupid job." He pushed the door open in a huff and, without looking at me, threw open the gate, got in the truck, and drove away.

Back in the house, I was sure Marion was crying, like she did so often lately. I picked the leash off the driveway and took it back to my crate with my blanket and ball.

Another chilly bedtime came and went, but that night Jim never came home. No one fed me breakfast or gave me water the next day. I felt like Jim as I sat by the side door, staring into the clouds. What was the use? Why did I have a family when I never saw them? Why was I alive when I had no life? I lived my days dreaming of better ones and spent my nights chasing rats. My life was lonely, and I wondered if it was ever going to improve.

Chapter Ten

Byron

Snow covered the ground and icicles hung from the gutters. The air was colder than I'd ever felt, and it didn't seem to be warming up. Lately, colorful lights had been strung all up and down our street, and people decorated their yards with plastic reindeer and snowmen. The excitement in our neighborhood was building, except at our house. It was the same as always.

The garage was still my home. Even though I had no warmth except for my body heat and Tommy's blanket, I still wasn't allowed inside the house. I had outgrown my crate and was sleeping on a pile of leaves that accumulated in the garage during the fall. My blanket, pink ball, and leash were right next to me. They gave me a sense of security throughout the long, cold nights.

Jim had all but forgotten about me. He practically threw my food into the garage to avoid walking over snow drifts that blocked the driveway. He was also bad about refilling my water, which froze solid almost every night. Luckily I learned to eat snow, which Jim should have been pleased with, but finding anything good about me wasn't his thing. The short amount of time he spent at home, he fought with Marion. Otherwise, she and the kids hid quietly inside the house and never made a peep. Only rarely did the boys play in the snow. When they did, they avoided the backyard because of all the dog piles I couldn't help but make.

Late one afternoon, Tommy stepped outside with no coat or shoes. There was no snow that day, but the ground was frozen and Tommy's breath smoked as it hit the air. I greeted him at the door and was excited to see him. He took me by the collar and led me into the garage. His small body shook from the cold, and he looked sad. Snuggling close to me, he sat down cross-legged on the dirt floor and wrapped his arms around me. With his voice small and vulnerable, he talked quietly into my ear.

"Byron, you and I are going to run away, okay? We have to find someplace else to live. I don't want to be here anymore." His words quivered, and he sniffled as he spoke. I felt wet where his face pressed against me. "Dad said Santa isn't coming tonight, and I don't even know what I did wrong!" He let go of my neck and looked at me. Tears dripped down his pink cheeks, and his lips were purple from the cold. "I thought about going to my grandma's house in Kansas, but she doesn't like dogs. Besides, she'd tell my mom. So I have to think of somewhere else."

He hugged my neck and buried his face again. His shoulders shuddered as he sobbed. I wondered where Steven was and if he would go with us. After all, the boys had relied on each other so much lately. Marion's attention was all on the baby, and Jim was never home.

Tommy noticed my leash in the corner and sat up tall, wiping his tears with his sleeves. "Oh, I was looking for that earlier. We're gonna need it." He reached back and grabbed the leash, stuffing it in his pocket. A bit more optimistic, he continued, "I know where your food is, so I'll pack that. I'll bring a blanket, a bottle of water, and your ball. Anything else we need, I'll think of it before tonight. Mom always hides granola bars behind the cereal, so I'll take a bunch of those. And, I have nine dollars in my wallet from my birthday."

I saw a plan forming in Tommy's head. There was nothing I'd rather do than run away from this dreary house with all of its problems, but I wasn't comfortable. I had gotten a little older, and my instincts told me it wasn't a good idea. Tommy was way too young, and I didn't know my way around the city. I hoped he would fall asleep that night and forget about it.

"Okay boy, I'll see you around midnight." Tommy kissed me on the head and ducked out of the garage.

That evening as it darkened, I could see through our fence that the neighborhood had come alive. It must have been a special night because decorations, laughter, and music spilled out of most of the houses. The later it got, the more cars parked on our street. There were pine trees in almost every window dressed with sparkling lights, candy canes, and strings of popcorn. Through front windows, people smiled as they unwrapped packages of red and green, hugging and kissing each other. Church bells rang from all around, and kids ran up and down the sidewalks throwing snowballs and wishing each other a "Merry Christmas."

Our house did nothing. I wasn't sure why we had to be so different all the time. The only thing about it that matched the rest of the neighborhood was the snowman on our front lawn. It was partially melted, but still stood upright with two sticks poking out of the middle and a hat on its head.

I barked hello at a few people that walked by and then I

went into the garage. A cold wind had picked up at dusk, and I couldn't stand to be outside more than the time it took to go potty. Although I was preoccupied with what Tommy had told me, it didn't stop me from feeling tired. Sleeping, I found, made the long nights go by faster. I curled into a tight ball, tucking my face under my warm, bushy tail. I listened to the distant laughter of neighbors and tried to ignore the silence that surrounded my own house. Before long, I fell into a deep sleep.

Chapter Eleven

Trudy

The dying woman knew it was her last Christmas. She was surprised that she had made it this far, but was delighted since Christmas was her favorite season. It was a time she could enjoy her family and share warm memories of her beloved husband who had passed not long ago.

As she thought about the presents she had bought her grandchildren, she realized she was already giving them the most precious gift of all—time. Her inheritance money had been divvied up, as well as a secret investment that one of them would enjoy when she was gone. But no matter how much of herself she gave, or the number of dollars she donated, nothing could reverse the selfish acts she committed years ago.

As she sat in the living room, staring at the Christmas tree with its twinkling ornaments and dancing lights, the old lady realized her portable oxygen tank was empty. She tried calling to her daughter, but was suddenly too out of breath to speak. As she went to ring the bell beside her arm chair, her body went limp and she collapsed. Whether it was the lack of oxygen or truly a horrible nightmare, memories of a past Christmas ran through her mind like a movie, going from wonderful to hellish as the woman slowly fell into a coma.

Byron

For some reason I hadn't dreamt since the night before I came to the Meloons. But on the night that Tommy planned to run away, it happened again.

It was Christmas Eve night as snow frosted over the window panes and wind whistled through the house. I lay by the fireplace at the foot of my owner. She wore soft black slippers that tucked under my body and held a glass with lipstick stains on the rim. Sitting in an elegant armchair painted in prints of red and gold, her dress was made of dark burgundy and forest green. She looked beautiful, emanating the rich colors of the season.

On the floor next to me was her daughter Julie, snuggled beneath a quilt. Across the room, sipping a soda, was my owner's husband who eyed me every now and then. Normally I lived outside in my doghouse. But on those bitter cold nights when my water froze and the snow was too deep to shovel, I was allowed to sleep in the kitchen. Since tonight was Christmas Eve, my family invited me to join them in the parlor.

Standing up to gather crumpled wrapping paper, Julie excused herself from her parents and left the room.

"Trudy," the man spoke after a long draw of his drink, "while we're sitting here, why don't we decide what we're going to do this summer." He glanced up at her while swirling his ice cubes. "Julie will graduate from college in the spring, and we can afford to move back to the city. The market is good for buying, and I have scouted an area just outside of Birmingham that I think you'll like."

Chapter Eleven

Trudy looked uncomfortable with the suggestion. She set her glass on the end table and leaned over to stroke my back. "I know you want to move, Clare. I know you're tired of your long commute and the dirt roads. But, we have Thor and—"

Clare held up his hand and stopped her in mid-sentence. "If it's about the dog, I don't want to hear it. We're not staying out here just because of a dog." He stood up and walked to the bar to refill his glass. "The dog will be happy, no matter where he is. He doesn't know the difference, and I refuse to take him with us."

I looked up to see Trudy's expression, and her eyes had filled with tears. She continued to stroke my back, while her feet moved nervously underneath me. She took a deep breath before continuing.

"Clare, honey, I know how you feel about taking him with us, but just think how many houses get robbed in the suburbs. Thor would be perfect there." She looked down at me, then back at her husband. "And you know he's never lived with anyone but us. How could you think he'd be okay with a stranger?"

I knew Trudy didn't like to beg. She was much too proud. But she had grown to love me as much as I loved her. I felt it in my soul. Thinking she could leave me broke my heart.

When Clare turned around he had changed. He had large black holes in the place of his eyes and pink wrinkled skin that stretched over his mouth. He looked our way, but I couldn't tell where his gaze fell. The holes squinted angrily, then he began to laugh, making a queer gurgling noise. Soon, the pink skin over his mouth ripped open, and teeth fell all over the floor. Black slime oozed from both nostrils, dripping into his torn mouth and spewing as he laughed. His cackles and howls became unbearably loud, and I felt the need to bury my head in Trudy's lap. But when I turned toward her, she was gone and her chair was covered in the black slime that Clare spat everywhere.

As he walked toward me, I tried to stand and found that I couldn't. The slime had buried my feet. When I looked around for an escape, I noticed that it poured from every crack and crevice in the room. Black bubbling goo seeped from the windows, the fireplace, and the doorways. It deepened around my torso until my entire body was covered except for my face.

I wasn't sure when Clare disappeared, but at some point I sat alone waiting to suffocate. The slime had crept over my nose, and I couldn't breathe anymore. From a distance, I heard a door creak and felt an ice-cold draft over the tips of my ears.

I woke up with a start to see Tommy's silhouette duck under the garage door. He walked toward me with his finger to his lips, whispering "shh."

Chapter Twelve

Byron

It was so cold that night that the water on my nose formed ice crystals as soon as I stepped onto the driveway. Looking at the sky, there was nothing but stars and a full moon. The wind had died to a calm, and Tommy's breath puffed white swirls in the frigid air. I was happy to see that he had dressed warmer than usual. He wore a knit hat, a bulky winter coat, jeans, and tennis shoes. His gloves hung out of his coat pocket, but at least he had them. My leash dangled from one of his hands, and his overstuffed backpack was slung heavily over his shoulders.

"Okay, boy, we're gettin' out of this place. Mom and Dad are sleeping, and we have all night to travel before they wake up and notice we're gone." As he spoke, he attached my leash.

I didn't wiggle or play because I wasn't excited to go. All I pictured was Jim waking up and finding us gone. That would send him into the biggest rage of his life. Not only would he be furious with Tommy, but he wouldn't trust me anymore. I was supposed to do what Jim said, not what Tommy said. To leave like this in the middle of the night felt very wrong. It was too dark, too quiet, and I didn't know where we were going. I wasn't sure I could protect Tommy and didn't believe he could protect me. We were leaving the only home we knew and venturing into the unknown with nothing but a backpack.

I looked out beyond the safety of the fence and saw colorful lights still glowing up and down our street. Car sounds from the main road were few and far between, but still heavy for this time of night. Marion repeatedly told the boys to stay away from "the highway." I was sure that's where we were headed as Tommy led me through the gate and turned toward the noises of the city.

"Well, Byron, this is what my plan is," he said, pulling wrinkled paper out of his pocket while we walked. "We're gonna go to the highway up there," he pointed with his bare finger, "and turn right. Then we're gonna walk to the bus stop at the corner and wait for the next bus. When the bus comes, I'll tell the driver that we're visiting my grandma who's blind and lives in Toledo, and that I have to deliver you to her house for Christmas. You're gonna be her new seeing-eye dog. Which, you know, you're really not gonna be. You'll stay with me." He breathed hard as he talked and fought to stay warm. "And then we're gonna drive to Toledo which is only about an hour away. And when we get there, we'll walk to the zoo, where my Uncle Bob lives. My dad said he fits in good behind bars with the other animals, so I know he'll love you. When we find him, I'm gonna tell him that we can't live at home anymore because my dad is a jerk. He doesn't like my dad either, so I know he won't call my parents."

Tommy looked satisfied with his plan. He shivered but didn't seem to notice the cold, which turned his cheeks red and made his nose drip.

When we got to the end of our street, Tommy paused for a minute and looked down at his piece of paper. After stuffing it back in a pocket, he placed his gloves on his trembling hands and led me onto the highway's cracked and beaten sidewalk.

I had driven down this road twice before, but never walked it. Whenever a truck sped past, I felt like it sucked me off the sidewalk. Sometimes two or three vehicles drove by at the same time. Tommy didn't flinch, but I cringed. Even though we weren't far from home, it was a whole different world out here. I didn't see any trees or shrubs. Streetlights, traffic lights, and headlights blinded me on and off as we walked. Smoke from manholes swirled like cotton into the air, and the decorations that made our neighborhood so colorful in the last several weeks didn't seem to brighten the busy roadway. If anything, it looked bad. Green roping drooped over the street lights, and gold and silver tinsel wrapped loosely around the telephone poles with half of it falling onto the sidewalk.

I kept pulling Tommy away from the curb, worried he would get hit by a car. But he tugged right back and seemed comfortable in the whirl of the speeding traffic. As we walked, his eyes focused directly ahead, and at one point, he ducked behind a bench and pulled me close.

"Sit, Byron. Don't move," he whispered as he stood still as a statue. I was confused until I saw the police car drive by. "Phew, that was close," he said with a sigh of relief.

We continued on our journey, Tommy still looking ahead. I became engrossed with all the life happening on the street around us. It was something I never got to see.

Several people sat eating by themselves in a diner. They looked lonely and sad as they stared at their newspapers or out the window. Cars pulled in and out of a gas station next door, while customers stood idly filling their tanks or wandered in and out of the convenience store. Next, we passed a fast food restaurant where cars pulled up one by one to a window and picked up delicious-smelling bags of food. Nearby a man in layers of torn, dirty clothing watched those cars while he picked through a dumpster. As I pitied the hungry man, a young underdressed woman standing on the corner giggled and approached Tommy.

"That's a cute puppy you have there," she said, showing several rotten teeth with lipstick stains.

"Thanks," replied Tommy, not looking at the woman.

"Where's your daddy, little boy?" she asked.

Tommy ignored her and walked faster, focusing his gaze on the sidewalk ahead.

When we got to the bus stop, he looked relieved. He sat down in the small glass shelter and held me close. An old lady sitting on the same bench talked nonsense with herself, never acknowledging us. I managed to stay warm because of my fur, but I saw that Tommy was freezing and his teeth were chattering.

"Byron, look. That sign over there says it's only twelve degrees outside. Wow, no wonder."

He stuck his face in my neck and I felt his body shiver. I wished we could just go home.

During a pause in the woman's conversation, I heard scuffling noises behind the shelter. They came from an alley between two vacant stores. I saw shadows move but couldn't tell what they were. They looked too big for rats and were definitely not humans. For a moment car lights captured a pair of eyes, and I growled. The sound startled Tommy.

"Byron, what is it, boy?" He turned to look in the same direction. His eyes squinted, and he shifted his body to get a better look. "I don't see anything. It's okay, boy, there's nothing there."

He turned back to watch for the bus, but I didn't move. My curiosity was too piqued by then, and I wanted to get a better look. Soon enough, another set of headlights caught the alley just so, and I saw everything that time. To my surprise, a pack of dogs sat huddled together against the wall, their eyes glowing red and scary. I pulled from Tommy and barked loud enough to hear my own echo. At the same time, Tommy stood and yanked me toward the curb.

"Come on, Byron, our bus is here!"

The lights disappeared and so did the dogs. A big bus straightened out alongside the curb and opened its door. I kept barking as Tommy yanked at my leash.

"Byron, shut up!"

He dragged me up the first step of the bus before I saw the driver. He was an older man with silver hair and deep wrinkles. His bushy eyebrows lifted as he studied Tommy and me. We were the only passengers.

"Where are you two going this time of night?" questioned the man whose voice was deep and gruff. His ice blue eyes scanned Tommy's face as he waited for an answer. I got the feeling he knew exactly what we were doing.

Tommy prepared to explain. He looked to the ground rather than at the man, and his fingers fidgeted with my leash. "Well sir, I'm taking my dog here to Toledo so he can be my grandma's leader dog. She's blind, and she's expecting us by morning—Christmas morning. We're supposed to spend the day with her."

The driver scratched his forehead, then turned to me. "Pretty puppy. Is he a German shepherd?"

"Yes sir," replied Tommy, shifting his weight from one foot to the other.

"Well, I'll tell you what, kid. This bus doesn't go directly to Toledo, but I can get you somewhere where you can connect. How does that sound?" His voice softened.

"Good, sir. Thank you, sir." Tommy pulled money out of his pocket and handed it to the driver.

The driver waved it off with a grunt and told him to go find a seat.

As I followed Tommy down the aisle, the man reached out and patted me tenderly on the head. By the way he touched me, I knew we'd be okay.

Tommy picked a seat three rows back and sat down. He put his arm around me and whispered, "We're on our way, boy. My story worked." He looked happy and relieved. I was relieved too, but for a different reason. My gut told me we were going home.

Chapter Thirteen

Clare

The man watched from the heavens as the boy and his dog walked off in the middle of the night. Even though he didn't approve of their home life, the world outside was much uglier, and the man knew he had to do something. He just wasn't sure how to communicate with the dog. Although the boy wasn't technically his problem, he loved kids and felt an obligation. The boy was just nine and the dog was his puppy.

After thinking for a while, the man remembered something a psychic told him during the war. His squadron had gone to see her one night after hearing spooky messages over their radio. The woman told them that spirits communicate through electrical energy and that their fallen comrades were just saying hello. At the time he thought it was nonsense, but now he believed anything was possible and figured he had nothing to lose.

As he watched the dog and boy step onto the bus, the man humbly requested help from his Almighty Father. He collected every bit of energy he could muster and went to work.

Byron

The bus pulled away from the curb and I looked outside for the dogs in the alley, but it was too dark. All I saw was the glass shelter and the woman who never got on the bus.

I wondered what it was about those dogs that attracted me. Maybe it was because I thought they were lucky to be free. They could do whatever they wanted, whenever they wanted. They didn't have to sleep alone, and they probably weren't afraid. They had each other.

As we drove down the highway, I noticed the driver fuss with his radio. After trying to talk into the handset, he put his ear to the speaker and looked at it confusedly. More than once, he turned the dial back and forth, shaking his head. He even banged on the device a couple times and still didn't seem satisfied.

"Huh? What the heck is going on?" He sat at a stoplight, staring at the radio. No matter what station he tuned to, the noise never changed. First there was just static. But when I listened more closely, a man's voice repeated the words, "Take them home. Take them home."

The driver turned his head to look at us, then back at the radio. The voice got clearer with each repetition. "Take them home."

"Take them..." the driver said to himself. He put his palm to his forehead and then checked it again with the back of his hand.

Tommy was oblivious to the driver. He probably dreamed of living in Toledo with his uncle, playing with me, or relaxing at the zoo. He looked out his window at passing traffic and seemed content in the warm vinyl seat. Not until we slowed to a stop did Tommy pay attention, which was understandable when he saw where we had parked.

Right in front of us were the police headquarters.

Tommy's face went from pacified to terrified. He stood up, looking from window to window and then at the bus driver. When the bus driver finally turned around again, he was also pale with beads of sweat on his forehead. For a moment, the two of them just stared at each other. The driver wiped his forehead, steadying himself on the armrest.

"Sorry, son, but I have no choice," said the man, catching his breath. "You belong home with your parents, or whoever you live with. Besides, my radio here is malfunctioning and I need to get it fixed before I can go any further."

Tommy sat back down. I knew what he was thinking, but I also knew the bus driver was right. In my opinion, he saved our lives.

Tommy began to sob uncontrollably. I moved as close to him as I could, watching two uniformed cops walk out of the station and stroll toward the bus. They climbed cautiously up the steps. One of them smiled sympathetically when he saw Tommy and me.

"What do we have here?" he said. His voice was soothing and I liked him.

The driver looked relieved. He wasn't so out of breath when he spoke again. "I picked these two up on the corner of Norman Highway and Scott Street. It would be awfully nice if you could find out where they live and take them home. I'm sure their parents will be glad to see them, especially on Christmas morning."

"We'll do our best," said the other cop while he motioned for Tommy to follow.

Tommy, still crying, stood up and walked toward the two officers. His hand shook as he held tightly to my leash. He didn't look at the driver or either of the officers as he stepped off the bus.

Before the lever doors shut behind us, I heard the driver's radio return to normal.

When Jim finally arrived at headquarters, Tommy didn't say a word. He had stopped crying before the officer made the phone call and sat frozen-faced ever since. If he could have blinked and made himself disappear, I'm sure that's what he would have done.

As for Jim, he made his feelings clear on the way home.

"What is wrong with you, boy? I have never been so embarrassed in front of my colleagues! What were you thinking in that feeble brain of yours?" Jim's lips quivered as he spoke. "Do you know what could have happened to you? Do you know what kind of people wander around in the middle of the night? Have you listened to anything I've ever taught you? You could have been seriously hurt. And worse, I'm going to have to explain to everyone why my son was trying to run away from home! You have shamed me, Tommy, and it's going to take a lot more than apologies to earn my trust back!"

Tommy didn't try to apologize. I wasn't sure if he'd ever talk to Jim again.

For me, life returned to normal the next day. Christmas came and went, with a bowl of food and some water. Jim told me over and over again how useless I was, since I had let Tommy out of the yard that night. When he had a security system installed later that week, I knew he had lost all faith in me.

"Here, you men should be able to install the alarm without my dog bothering you," explained Jim as he tied me to the tree. "He's harmless."

The workmen didn't seem to think so, especially when I barked. They steered clear of me the whole time they worked in the yard.

"Geez, I wonder why this guy's payin' for a system when he's got a big dog like that," said one of them.

"Beats the tar outta' me," said the other. "Maybe he's sick. He doesn't look too good. I can see his ribs stickin' out through his fur."

"Yeah, could be," agreed the first one.

Until that day, I hadn't thought of myself as a big dog, a sick dog, or a skinny dog. I knew I had grown because I was tall enough to see inside the kitchen without jumping. I also noticed that my crate only came to my chest. When I put my paws on the fence I was able to look over with no effort, and I was tall enough to kiss Steven's face. Being skinny wasn't a big deal either. I was used to myself that way and had a lot of energy. I just wished Jim trusted me more. No matter what I did, I figured he would always think of me as a failure.

As much as I loved the boys, winter dragged on and I started to think how nice it would be to live on the streets like those other dogs. I had many opportunities to escape, but every time I thought about it, I felt guilty. I had a responsibility to my family that I couldn't ignore. Even though Jim didn't trust me, I remained his watchdog to the best of my ability. I barked at the mailman every day, and I patrolled the fence in the wind, rain, and snow. I had to prove to my family that I was a good dog. Besides, I had become quite territorial and needed to guard my property.

For the most part, the garage protected me throughout the winter. There were still snow drifts that crept under my door and drops in temperature that caused me to wonder if I would survive. But if it hadn't been for the garage, I'm sure the wind would have done me in. Even though I didn't feel lucky, I was thankful for my shelter.

One day I woke up to singing birds and sunshine. Scents of mud, worms, and new grass permeated the air. To my amazement, spring had snuck up. For the first time since fall, I felt warm.

Marion walked from window to window, opening each one. Stale air from inside the house drifted outside, and the smell reminded me of when I first got to the Meloons'. I also heard the boys' voices for the first time since winter. It was comforting to hear Tommy. He hadn't been outside since Christmas. In fact, no one ever left the house anymore except to go to school. When they did, Jim had to turn the alarm off.

"Beep, beep, beep—disarmed, disarmed," a strange voice would say.

With the windows open, came also the sounds of unhappiness. Steven's temper tantrums worsened, and Andrew screamed nonstop. Somehow Marion had also changed. Not only did she yell at the boys more, but one day she actually talked to me. As she cleaned the kitchen window, she stopped suddenly and stared.

"Oh my God, look at you. I thought he loved you more than the rest of us, but apparently not." She shook her head and went back to her work.

When summer began again, I hoped things would go back to normal. I wanted the boys to throw the ball and talk under the tree again. But Tommy only came out on the driveway a few times a day. Nobody played in the backyard anymore because dog dirt stuck on their shoes and smeared in the house, complained Marion. Besides, the grass was too long, and it made Tommy itch.

As the days got hotter, I spent as much time as I could by the kitchen door. That part of the driveway stayed cool until lunchtime, and I was comforted hearing Marion and the boys in the morning. One day while Tommy and Steven were at a friend's, I heard Marion on the phone.

"No, Mom, he doesn't know anything yet," she said quietly, and then paused. "Because you know Jim, and he's not going to take it well. Honestly, I'm a little afraid for the boys. They're going to have enough to deal with." She paused again. "Yep, the moving truck will be here on August twentieth, and the boys and I will be on the train that afternoon."

I couldn't believe what I heard. By the way she talked, it sounded like she and the boys were moving away! I was shocked. Even worse, Jim didn't know. I sat there and took it all in. *The boys and I will be on the train that afternoon.* I realized she hadn't mentioned me. What did Marion plan to do with me? I doubted I would go with them, the way she hated me.

But with Tommy gone, I didn't know what I'd do. I couldn't imagine life without him. He was the only person who loved me or cared what happened to me. And how was Jim going to manage? Jim couldn't take care of himself anymore. The only time he even looked alive was when he yelled. How would he react when he found out his whole family was leaving?

As the days went on, I listened to Marion's conversations. There was no talk between her and the boys, and Jim couldn't have known anything because he carried on as usual. The only thing that changed was Marion. Every morning after Jim left, she would brave her way into the garage and deposit another box. If I tried to approach her, she would jump and scream "No!" She must have known that Jim never went in there anymore, because she wouldn't have taken that chance. Day after day, the boxes collected in the darkest corner until they were almost to the rafters. Jim and the boys never saw them. I, on the other hand, was devastated as I stared at the boxes, knowing Tommy would soon go with them.

Chapter Fourteen

Trudy

Ever since the old woman awakened from her coma, she hadn't been the same. Only minor brain damage had occurred from the hypoxia, but she knew she lived on borrowed time. Most of her day was spent staring out her window from a hospital bed—one that her children insisted she have in her bedroom.

What disturbed the woman most was the nightmare she had experienced right before she lost consciousness. For the first time, her husband was involved in the cruelty toward the dog, and she remained haunted by those images every day. Thankfully she hadn't dreamt since, and what a relief that those horrible things hadn't really occurred. Or had they? She honestly couldn't remember. Was her pain medication playing tricks on her, or was she the monster her nightmares portrayed her to be?

As the woman lay unable to sleep, she remembered that it was her wedding anniversary. Seventy years ago that day, August twentieth, she and her beloved husband were married with God as their witness. After being a faithful wife for all those years until his death, she had always hoped that their souls would bond forever in heaven. Maybe he waited for her. Maybe he guided her as she asked for forgiveness and journeyed to the other side. Oh, how wonderful it would be to see him again!

Overtaken by sweet memories of past celebrations, the woman fell asleep. Unfortunately she was rudely reminded that hell wasn't as far away as she thought.

Byron

Marion got busier. Moving day must have been close, but since nobody seemed to know anything about it, life at the Meloon's stayed the same. Of course, I wasn't the same. I felt more insecure than ever. I rarely left the kitchen door, and I slept poorly, listening for signs of anything in the middle of the night. I wished I had known when August twentieth was, but dates didn't make sense to me. All I knew was that Marion and the boys were moving soon.

I walked slowly into the garage and looked at the boxes. A pit grew in my stomach as I thought about what was happening. It didn't seem real to think that I would never see Tommy or feel his hugs again. No one would smile at me or wave to me from inside the house. I wouldn't hear laughter in the morning or dishes clinking in the kitchen. It would all be gone. The only things I would have were my ball, my ripped blanket, and my garage.

I fell into a restless sleep and began dreaming of the home I had dreamt of so many times before. I was consciously aware that my brain slipped toward that place and tried to wake myself up, but for some reason I couldn't. As I dropped deeper into the mysterious life of Thor, it became less fantasy and more reality. Then I was there.

Chapter Fourteen

I walked side by side with my beautiful owner, Trudy. She loved me and I adored her. She had become such a big part of my life that I felt her in my soul. Once she assured me that we would be together no matter where we were in this world, and I believed her. She was all that I had and all that I needed. We were equals, and I trusted her with my life.

As we walked around the far side of the pond, I mentally prepared for our hunt. Trudy and I made a good team. I used my nose and she used her eyes as we scouted for a large snapping turtle that she would cook for dinner. The dish had always been a delicacy, and tonight would be a perfect night for it. It was their wedding anniversary, and Clare said he had good news.

Looking into the water we saw our reflections, and Trudy smiled at me. There were no ripples or bugs, and the only noises were our footsteps crunching lightly in the reeds. As our heads canvassed the depths of the pond, the grasses to our right swayed suddenly. We both turned and saw a large, slow turtle making its way toward the edge of the pond. I looked at Trudy for permission, and she glanced back as if to say, "Go ahead, get him." As quickly and quietly as I could, I pounced on the thing. It swung its long grotesque head to bite me, and Trudy stepped on the creature's neck, breaking it with skill. When it finally stopped struggling, she picked up the dead weight of the turtle and we carried it proudly back to the house.

When we entered the kitchen, the phone rang. Trudy answered it. "Okay, Clare. I'll expect you later then." She looked disappointed. "I love you, too."

She hung up the phone and glanced over at me. "Well, it's just you and me for a while again, boy."

Trudy prepared her dinner as I lay by her feet, waiting for scraps. She tossed a couple of bloody webbed feet in the air, and

I caught them with no problem. As I waited for the best part, saliva watered my mouth and dripped to the floor. Trudy smiled at me, knowing exactly what I anticipated. Slowly, she lifted the butcher's knife and slammed it down on the counter, chopping the turtle's head off. I stood to accept my treat, putting my nose right up to the counter. As if to tease me, she picked up the slimy head and threw it toward the ceiling. When it came down, rather than falling to the floor, it froze in the air and bobbed lifelessly in front of my face. As it hung before me, it suddenly came to life. It opened its eyes and then its mouth and breathed in short raspy spurts. Trudy continued to dig the rest of its body out of the shell, oblivious to my situation. As I looked to her for help, the head spoke to me.

"You are going to be alone," it said in a wet, garbled voice. "You will die alone."

It snapped its mouth wider with each word. The bloodshot eyes bore into me like fiery darts as it warned me of my own death. I backed away and turned to avoid the monster, but its ugly face kept appearing in front of me. I barked for Trudy, but no sound came out. Where did she go? Why did she leave me?

I woke up then to the sound of a door and realized where I was. Forgetting about my nightmare, I ran out to the driveway as Jim threw my food onto the pavement. He got in his truck and sped away.

Within minutes, I heard Marion bustling around in the kitchen. The whole time she worked, she spoke to herself.

"Okay, I can't forget that. Oops, I almost forgot that. Okay, I'm doing fine. Fine, fine, fine. Gotta get the boys up now."

Her feet banged up the stairs, and I heard her go into the boys' rooms. Andrew started to cry, and Steven's voice whined through the window. "Mom, go away. I'm too tired."

"Steven, honey, you have to get up."

Then I heard Tommy's voice. "Mom, what are you doing? Why are you putting my stuff in a suitcase?" There was a pause. "Mom, where are we going?"

"Just get up, Tommy. I need your help. We're going to visit Grandma, and we're leaving this morning. You have to get up now."

"Wait, what about Dad and Byron?" he asked sleepily.

"Dad and Byron will be fine while we're gone. Let's go."

As Marion lied to the boys and settled Andrew, I heard a large truck turn down our street. It stopped in front of our house, and two bulky men stepped down from the cab. As they walked toward the gate, I jumped up and barked. The loud noise startled the men and one of them tripped, putting his hand to his chest.

"Holy matrimony! Check my pulse; that's a big dog!" he cried.

They collected themselves and turned toward the front door. I heard Marion say from around the corner, "The boxes are in the garage. My son will come out and hold the dog so you can get them."

Reluctantly, the men came back around, keeping their distance from the gate. They stood and waited as Tommy exited the side door, looking baffled. Tommy saw me and then noticed the two movers. "Why is there a moving truck here?" he asked. He walked to where I stood on the gate and put his hand on my head. "It's okay, Byron. Stop barking."

I didn't stop. There was no way I would let those movers take my family away. Each time they tried to come closer, I barked louder and threw my body at the gate. The fence rattled and clanked, and the movers backed away.

Tommy grabbed my collar and pulled. "Byron, get down! Byron, COME!"

The movers watched with open mouths as Tommy yanked me hard. Slobber dripped from my mouth and onto the driveway as I fought and choked. I started to feel angry at Tommy and couldn't understand why he was on their side.

"Byron, NO!" he yelled again. I turned my head abruptly to stop him from hurting me and when I did, my teeth accidentally banged into his face. Blood poured from the large gash in his cheek. Marion stepped outside at that moment and screamed, as the movers looked on with horror.

"Stop that dog, for God's sake! Get him away from my boy!"

Tommy let go of me and put his hand to his face. When he realized he was bleeding, he cried out loud, which only added to Marion's hysteria. The movers charged the fence to grab me while Marion rushed Tommy in the house. As they fumbled with the latch on the gate, I thought fast. It was obvious that I had to get out of there, but I wasn't sure how. The two men blocked the gate, and there was no other escape from the backyard. I did the only thing I could think of. I circled around behind the garage and gathered all the speed I could muster. From the back fence, I raced toward the gate. The movers saw me coming and hopped out of the way. Their eyes widened with fear and their faces went white. With one leap and a lot of faith, I soared over the fence and landed way beyond where they stood.

As I ran through the front yard, I couldn't sense anyone following me and was too afraid to look back. I ran down the sidewalk and through a couple of front lawns, following the path that Tommy took me down on Christmas Eve. It looked different because it was light outside. The ground was warm, and the trees had leaves. I felt more confident as my feet lifted off the ground in swift, long strides, carrying me toward the highway. For the first time, I felt free to run like Mama. The wind was strong in my face, and there was no fence to stop me. The only thing I didn't like was that I was alone and didn't have a plan. At that moment, my goal was to get as far away from the movers as I could. After that I would go to the bus stop and try to find those dogs.

As I got to the highway, I slowed down and turned right. I ran through driveways and behind buildings so no one could see me. People on foot avoided me, and cars screeched to a halt as I crossed in front of them. Despite the traffic, noise, and strangeness of the city, I didn't stop. I thought of what I had just done and the entire last year of my life. I felt like nothing more than a failure. As I approached the bus stop, I looked toward the alley and wondered if the dogs were there.

Chapter Fifteen

Clare

The man from heaven had to think fast again. It looked like the dog had just bitten the little boy and was running away from the house. He understood why the dog needed to leave. But again, life was much worse on the streets. Somehow the man needed to get the dog back home until he could think of an alternative plan. Where was his wife when he needed her? She would have known what to do.

As he watched the dog run alongside the highway, he was drawn to a strange energy nearby. He scanned the area from above, trying to find its origin. Somehow he kept returning to a homeless man rummaging through a dumpster. When he honed in on the man to study him more closely, the garbage picker dropped what he was doing and turned around. He looked to the right and to the left. Putting his face to the heavens, he raised his hands in frustration, and said, "What do you want?" The angel was thrilled—the homeless man felt him too.

Byron

When I got to the alley, there was no one there. Food wrappers littered the ground, and the smell of urine and cigarettes hung in the humid morning air. I had to be careful where I stepped so I wouldn't cut my feet on broken glass. In the corner of one of the buildings was a torn, dirt-stained backpack that overflowed with clothing and plastic bottles.

As I sniffed the empty alleyway, a ragged-looking man stumbled into the corner and sat on the ground next to the backpack. He stuffed a bag of half-eaten fries and a bottle of half-drunk soda into the pack and sat against the wall. Either he didn't see me or he didn't care. He rested his head against the bricks and closed his eyes.

When I began to move again he jumped, grabbing the bag. Seeing me standing there, the man froze. "Easy boy, easy," he slurred in a shaky voice. He sat stiff as cardboard, clutching his backpack in front of him, as the whites of his eyes popped out from behind his filthy bearded face.

I didn't move either. I was still afraid that someone would catch me, and I didn't want to cause any more trouble. Staying far away from the man, I continued to sniff. But all I could smell was his unwashed body from several feet away. There were no signs of another dog, and I wasn't sure where else to look. The shaded alley seemed like a good place to hide for the time being. It was out of view and felt safe enough except for the man. So, I picked a spot opposite him and lay down.

As I rested my body, my mind went back to Tommy. I wondered if his face hurt and if he hated me. I would probably never know and was sure I'd never see him again. We didn't even have a chance to say goodbye. I already missed my Tommy.

The man in the corner began to fidget. First it seemed like he slept soundly. But the more I watched him, the more restless he became. He turned his head from side to side and up and down. Then he squinted strangely and focused on me. Although I tried to avoid direct eye contact, it was hard. His blue eyes burned right through me.

"Someone's tryin' to send you a message, and it's messin' up my thoughts," he said.

His food-stained mustache moved as he talked, and I figured he must be speaking to someone else. His face looked irritated, and he shook his head nervously. As creeped out as I was, I couldn't ignore him.

"He said he's watchin' out for you until Trudy dies."

What did he just say? That time I lifted my head and stared back. He swatted flies from his nose.

"Go home," he stated firmly, still piercing me with his eyes.

What? Home where? Who was he talking about, and why did he mention Trudy? Was it the Trudy from my dreams? And if so, how did he know about her?

He wiped his sweaty brow and looked away. Squeezing his eyes shut, he sat back against the wall humming loudly. Several times he changed the position of his feet and shifted his weight. But the man couldn't seem to get comfortable. He covered his ears and rocked back and forth, looking like he was about to explode. Finally he did.

"Oh for God's sake, go away! Go home, dog! I can't take this guy's noise anymore! If you're lucky enough to have a home, then go back to it!"

That was enough for me. I got up and ran out of the alley. From behind the buildings, I turned right and headed toward the house. Although I had no intention of going home, I didn't know where else to go. I looked for places to hide, but there were only dumpsters that smelled of rotten trash lining the narrow back alley.

When the passage opened up to a parking lot, there was the same fast food restaurant Tommy and I passed the night we ran away. The scent of cooking meat took me back, and I thought of how determined Tommy was to leave home. I guessed he was getting his chance now, and I should have been happy for him. Instead, I only felt sad for myself.

Out of the corner of my eye, I saw something move across the parking lot. I realized it was a dog. She crept awkwardly nearer until she reached the dumpster. There, she began to eat off the pavement and didn't notice me until I approached her. She was thin, white, and filthy.

"Hi," I said carefully, walking behind her to sniff.

Immediately her ears went back, and she showed her teeth. Her tail went between her legs, and an ugly growl escaped her mouth. Only for a moment did she look into my eyes. When she did, I saw fear.

"This is my food. Get away from me," she hissed as she swallowed half-eaten packages of food which swarmed with flies and maggots. She must have been hungrier than I ever imagined. I noticed her ribs through the thick, matted fur on her sides. Bugs crawled in her ears and over her nose, and she limped slightly.

Suddenly she whirled around and lunged, causing me to fall back on my hind legs.

"Go away!" she snarled.

"I'm sorry." I cowered as I turned around and walked back the way I came. I sat next to one of the rancid dumpsters and watched the dog as she continued to eat. After several minutes, a restaurant employee walked out the back door carrying a trash bag. When he saw the white dog, he stomped his feet and clapped his hands.

"Get out of here, you mutt! Get! Get!" He ran toward her, took the bag of trash and threw it, hitting her in the back. With her tail between her legs, she scurried away from the dumpster and out of sight.

My hopes dwindled as she disappeared behind a car. Although she wanted nothing to do with me, she was another dog, and I found that comforting. I could have followed her, but I would have had to cross the parking lot. I thought maybe I could go back to the homeless guy, but he scared me with his crazy talk. If only I could find those other dogs. They wouldn't mind an extra companion. And if they did, I would just have to learn to survive alone.

Chapter Sixteen

Kenny

Kenny was homeless. His luck had always been bad as a child, and when he grew up it got even worse. He had a bad habit of listening to people that weren't there, especially when they talked about animals. Some doctors told him he was schizophrenic; others told him he had a gift. Most people just thought he was crazy.

Years ago, Kenny worked as a veterinary assistant. He had always thought working with animals was his thing and was so excited when the vet offered him his dream job. After being there for a while, voices began to tell him stories about the patients. Kenny listened to them and helped solve problems that the vets couldn't even figure out. One day after being interrogated by his boss, Kenny proudly admitted his special ability and was fired. No one gave him a job after that, and his family disowned him. Kenny had nowhere to go but the streets.

No matter what he did, Kenny couldn't shut the voices up. Day after day, invisible people bugged him for favors. They needed help with this dog or that cat. At one point in his life it made him feel good, but the voices had ruined everything. The day the older man's voice asked him to help the German shepherd, Kenny flipped out. As bad as he felt, enough was enough. He just wanted to be left alone.

Byron

I sat by the dumpsters for most of the morning and wondered what to do. When the sun got too hot, I walked back toward the alley to find shade. Seeing the homeless guy still there, I continued on until the narrow road dead-ended at some railroad tracks. There, next to the tracks, was a dilapidated two-story building with a concrete porch extending off the back door. The building looked vacant, but I heard some noises under the porch. They sounded like dogs. *Finally*, I thought and took a deep breath.

I moved closer to the porch as quietly as I could. There was a small hole under the steps, so I stuck my head in it to get a better idea of who was in there. Suddenly a fury of barking, growling, and snapping exploded from the hole. Vicious faces drooling gobs of saliva bombarded me as I jumped back and ran across the road. I stood pinned against the railroad fence as several large dogs climbed out from under the porch and approached me, dropping their tails and showing their teeth. I was terrified. How could I have been so stupid? I should have known better than to trespass.

As they emerged one by one, they formed a semicircle around me. There were mostly big dogs, but a few little dogs stood among them, looking just as mean. All of them were matted and dirty, with flies in their ears and crust on their muzzles. I remained still, unsure of what they would do.

After what seemed like forever, a medium-sized dog

stepped through the semicircle and approached me. He sniffed under my tail and came around to my face. His voice was stern.

"I'm Rufus, and you have trespassed onto our property. State your business, shepherd. Why have you come here?"

I had to sniff him before I responded.

"My name is Byron, and I'm lost. I left my home this morning, and I'm sure my owner won't accept me back. I need help."

The alpha male spoke again. "What kind of help are you looking for? We're homeless and have nothing to offer."

"I just need some company," I said. "And I might need water later. I'm very thirsty."

Rufus looked at me thoughtfully and then turned to the rest of the pack. They conferred for a moment.

"Okay," Rufus said. "We agree you can join us, even though our accommodations are limited."

I was so happy. "Thank you, all of you. I'm so grateful."

The rest of the dogs came closer to sniff and say hello. Some of them were nice, and some looked annoyed. I understood and stayed with the nice ones.

When we got back under the porch, I was amazed. Rufus had been right when he said the accommodations were limited. Although very snug, it was still a nice home. They had collected blankets, pillows, stuffed animals, balls, and bones. Their hole in the ground had more things than my garage ever would, and they all seemed fairly happy.

After a nice long nap, I asked a small dog named Maya where she got water. I hadn't had a drink since last night, and all I could think about was my thirst.

"We never go out until dark, and then we get water at a couple different places," she explained. "There's a leaky faucet down the road behind a restaurant. Sometimes there are scraps of food there too. And then there's a big building across the highway that has a broken sprinkler system. Water drips off the roof and into the parking lot. We love going there, but it's dangerous crossing the highway. Last winter someone got hit, and twice Animal Control came and took a few of us. We have to be really careful."

"What happens when Animal Control takes someone?" I asked.

Maya thought for a minute. She looked around to see if anyone else could answer my question. "We're not sure. They never come back, and that's all we know."

"Crazy Kenny once said they take 'em to the pound and kill 'em," interjected one of the bigger dogs named Carlos.

Maya laughed. "And you really believe what he says?" she asked nervously.

"Hey, that guy knows everything," said Rufus. "It's pretty darned scary."

"He's full of bologna," said Maya.

"Why, because he told you your puppies were happy in heaven? He was just trying to make you feel better, Maya. He wasn't trying to be mean," replied Rufus.

"My puppies are not dead!" screamed Maya.

"Whatever," said Rufus. He looked toward the ceiling and rolled his eyes. Maya got up and squeezed past us with a huff. She went to the opposite corner and lay down.

"Who's Crazy Kenny?" I asked.

"Oh, he's this homeless guy that hears voices from heaven," answered Carlos. "He's not a bad guy, but he can really lose his temper. And a lot of the dogs don't want to hear what he has to say. He scares them."

"I think I met him today," I said, feeling excited that I could be a part of the conversation. "He told me to go home. I thought he was going to chase me right out of the alley."

"Yeah, he's done that before," said Rufus.

"Well, I didn't do what he said, and I had no idea what else he was talking about. But I have to admit, he scared me a little." I thought back to what he said about Trudy. *He's watchin' out for you until Trudy dies.* It was all a little too weird.

Carlos said, "I was glad I met Kenny because I found out why my owner left me." He got comfortable while the rest of the dogs yawned. "You see, one day I waited for him to get home from work and he never did. For days I sat alone in my house with no food and no way to get out. Finally some policemen came and when they saw me, they called Animal Control to take me to the pound. Well, I didn't know what that meant, but it had to be something bad. So I got past them and ran out the door." He paused a little and took a deep, thoughtful breath. "On the streets, I kept thinking my owner deserted me, and I was really mad and lonely. Then I met Crazy Kenny. I didn't ask for his help, but he blurted out that my owner had been murdered and was sorry he left me. He told me my owner loved me and to stay away from the cops and the Animal Control guy." Maya sighed from across the room. "That's when Crazy Kenny told me that it's true dogs are killed at the pound. He knew because he used to work for a vet, and he said that's what happened to strays when nobody took them home."

I listened closely to Carlos's story and wondered what else Crazy Kenny knew about Trudy. Maybe I should have gone home when he told me to. Besides, after listening to the other dogs, I was even more afraid of being caught. I didn't want to go to the pound. The question was, what would Jim do with me? Would he be mad at me? Or, would he be so devastated about his family leaving that he wouldn't even notice me? Maybe he needed comfort right now, like he did when his friend died. It was hard to know with Jim. All I knew was that it was getting dark outside, and I was afraid to be alone. I would stay with my new friends at least for the night. In the morning, I would decide what to do.

We stepped outside into the hot, humid darkness and stretched. Everyone sniffed along the fence and went potty. We hung around for a while then headed toward the restaurant with the leaky faucet. Surprisingly, no one complained about hunger.

"No one really feels like eating when it's hot like this," said Maya. "We're always hungrier in the winter, but then it's harder to find food."

As we walked down the back road, keeping an eye out for police cars, we passed the alley. The other dogs sped up to avoid being noticed, but I stopped.

There he sat. Kenny had been joined by a couple of other people. They talked casually until Kenny suddenly closed his mouth and looked around. His two companions grew quiet and asked, "What is it, Crazy Kenny? What do you hear? Is it my papa talkin'? Is my granny tellin' you she left me a million bucks?" They laughed, but Kenny ignored them and swatted at the air in front of his face. He turned his head to the side and leaned into the ground with his hands over his ears.

I moved nearer to the small group until I was in their line of vision. Kenny's friends stared at me wide-eyed and backed closer to the wall. They held their hands in front of them. "We don't have nothin' for you, big doggie. Go back where you came from." I ignored them and crept toward Kenny. He still didn't see me, but I knew he sensed me. After hearing his friends, he looked up from his crouched position and pounded his fist on the ground.

"GO HOME!" he screamed. "He's tellin' you to GO HOME! Trudy's dying, and he wants you back where you belong! Get out of here! Get away from me!"

He kicked his feet and put his hands back over his ears. I wanted to ask him who was telling me to go home, but I didn't know how.

When he started to get up, I turned and ran. I bolted past my new friends and through the fast food parking lot. Not stopping to catch my breath, I crossed over some driveways, ran along the busy highway, and onto my street. Once I turned the corner, I plopped down on some green grass and cried. I was so exhausted, and I knew there was no turning back. I had nothing but a crazy man's words. But for some reason, I believed him. Whoever sent me those messages had a reason, and going home seemed like my best alternative. Hopefully, Jim would be happy to see me.

Chapter Seventeen

Jim

When Jim got home, the house was empty. His wife and kids were nowhere to be found. In both bedrooms, the drawers had been emptied and the suitcases were missing. Jim was at a loss.

His first instinct was to call the police, but he was the police. Then he thought to call Marion's mother, but she had never liked him and Jim knew she wouldn't tell him the truth. Throughout his whole marriage, he had supported and cared for his family. He had paid the bills, put food on the table, and kept a roof over their heads. Jim had never cheated or lied. He had been the best husband and father he knew how to be. And this was how Marion repaid him? Jim slammed shut the empty drawers and stomped back down the stairs.

Then he remembered the dog. He realized the gate had been open when he pulled in the driveway and that the dog hadn't greeted him. When he went back outside and looked, the dog wasn't there. Marion surely wouldn't have taken him. She hated Byron. The stupid canine must have seen his chance and taken off.

Thinking he couldn't be too far away, Jim called for Byron. He went back to the garage and filled the food and water bowls to the top, feeling guilty that the dog probably hadn't eaten in a while. He folded a torn blanket he didn't recognize and lay it in the corner. Then he placed a pink squeaky ball next to the blanket and hoped Byron would return within the next few minutes. Jim felt desperate for someone to ground him, and the dog was his only hope. If the dog didn't come home, Jim had nothing left to live for.

Walking back inside the house, Jim flipped the light on and locked the kitchen door. He walked quietly upstairs to his bedroom and shut the door.

Byron

When I got back to the house, the gate was wide open and Jim's truck was in the driveway. Surprisingly, the kitchen light was on, even though it was so late. I sneaked under the garage door and saw a fresh bowl of water and a full bowl of food. I couldn't have been happier. After drinking every drop and eating every kibble, I thought about the friends I had left on the streets who still searched for their next meal. I also remembered the dog who ate from the dumpster that morning and wondered why she lived alone. I had forgotten to ask my new friends about her.

As I decided what to do next, I noticed that the boxes were gone and the garage was strangely empty. The boys came to mind, and I was suddenly filled with sadness again. After staring at the vacant corner for a minute and wondering if Tommy was happy, I went over to where my blanket had been laid out neatly and fell asleep with my ball tucked under my chest.

That night I had no trouble sleeping, but my dream was unsettling. I dreamt that I lived back on the streets, but this time with the hungry white dog from the dumpster. We slept in the alley with some homeless people who fed us pieces of their feet as they crumbled off. The dog and I were strangely happy and never felt hungry or lonely. As disgusting as it was, I didn't wake up feeling scared like my other dreams, but guilty that I had been given food and water that day. I wished so badly that I could go back to the alley and bring everyone home with me, but I knew that Jim would never tolerate it.

When the sun rose, I waited nervously for Jim to come outside with my food. I sat by the kitchen listening for noises within the house but heard nothing. I wondered if he was even home. The door appeared locked, and the kitchen light was still on. I supposed Jim could have gone out with a friend last night, leaving his truck at home. But that didn't fit because Jim didn't have any friends. I thought then that maybe he was so upset about his family that he couldn't get out of bed. But that didn't make sense either. I had never known Jim to miss work no matter how upset he was. After waiting by the door until late afternoon, I gave up and went back in the garage for a nap.

Later that day it started to rain. I was glad, because I was thirsty. I pushed my bowl under the downspout and collected water from the gutters. It would have been nice to have food, but I'd done without it so many times, I knew I would be okay.

As the sky darkened toward evening, I went back to the kitchen door and listened for Jim again. Nothing had changed since early morning, and I started to worry. At one point, the phone rang and no one answered. I heard the machine pick up and record a voice from police headquarters, asking Jim to return the call. Thinking maybe Jim heard the phone, I jumped against the door. But nothing moved and nothing changed.

Dusk turned to dark, and thunder built in the distance. The low rumbling noise, which never bothered me before, felt spooky. The boys always said it was just the angels bowling in heaven, but they weren't there to comfort me and I felt unsettled. I went back into the garage and tried to sleep, but every time I closed my eyes the thunder shook me awake and my stomach filled with butterflies. The gate was still open, so I had the option of going back on the streets. But Kenny's words came back to mind, and somehow I knew I needed to be at home.

I waited and watched, paralyzed by the heavy air that closed in around me. Static electricity from the approaching storm buzzed in my bones. The wind picked up and tree limbs swayed like goblins, scraping their claws across the garage roof. Small branches snapped off the trees and landed on the driveway, swirling among leaves and other debris. Between wind gusts and thunder, the air was eerily silent. Something felt terribly wrong. Every few minutes, a burst of lightning would illuminate the yard, making every leaf on every tree visible. The house would glow its sickly yellow-green color for that split second, overpowering the small light that shone from the kitchen window. Then a crashing sound more violent than I'd ever heard would catch me off guard and shake the ground. At one point a loud siren wailed in the distance, blending with the howling noises of the wind. Then it started to pour.

The rain poured so hard, I wondered if the garage would hold up. There had always been a leak near the back wall, but during heavy rains, water steadily drizzled in and formed a puddle by my crate. I picked up my blanket and moved it toward the front of the garage. Then I went back for my ball. If the roof caved in, I wanted at least those two things.

Chapter Seventeen

It seemed that hours passed as I stood anxious. The siren had stopped, but the rain continued, and the wind blew even stronger. All the lights in the neighborhood went out, and it seemed that a storm cloud stalled right over our house. The kitchen had become ghostly black without the small light, and I thought about breaking a window to find Jim. As I was just about to take my first step out of the garage, something unthinkable happened. My body went numb as I watched the telephone pole in the front yard get hit by a bolt of lightning. In slow motion, the pole broke in half, making a sick moaning sound as it fell in the direction of the front porch. Its electrical wires ripped halfway to the ground, shooting sparks and flames from the flailing uncoiled ends. The loose wires flung everywhere as the pole went straight for the house. The moment it hit, I knew it was all over. The flaming wires crashed through the living room window, and the entire house went up in a big orange ball. One by one the windows shattered as their fragments exploded into the yard. Black smoke poured from every loose brick and board, while fire licked and spit against the rain and wind. Sirens approached in the distance. Neighbors came outside to see what happened, holding umbrellas and staring in disbelief.

I had to get out of the garage because the flames were blowing in my direction, throwing sparks and debris under the door. I grabbed my ball and stepped onto the driveway, feeling a blast of hot air singe the fur around my face. As much as I hated the thought of Jim being in the house, there was nothing I could do to save him. I ran until I was completely off of our property and stood motionless watching the rest of my life burn to the ground. Nobody noticed me like I wished they would. I would have liked someone to tell me what to do.

But the neighbors were busy deciding if someone was trapped inside, yelling to each other over the roar of the fire. Rumors went back and forth among the women, while the men stood shaking their heads. When the fire trucks finally got there, the family's house was so far gone that nobody would ever know anything.

As the crowd of people cleared the yard and the firefighters finished their job, a couple of men carried a large black bag from the house out to an ambulance. They strapped it to a stretcher and closed the ambulance doors.

When the red glow of morning finally peered over the horizon, the temperature had cooled considerably and tired policemen strung yellow tape around the house. It was then that I saw a neighbor point me out to an officer close by. I stood next to a bush with my ball at my feet as he walked slowly toward me. When he smiled, I recognized his face immediately.

"Well, hello again, Byron. I figured I'd find you sooner or later. Are you okay?" His voice was calming and gentle. He let me sniff his hand and then he looked at the tag on my collar. He petted my head while he talked.

"Wow, you've really grown since Christmas. Do you remember me? My name is Mike. We met at the police station when your brother tried to steal you off to Toledo." He chuckled. "I'll never forget that."

Standing up, he looked down at my face. I looked back shyly, wagging my tail and holding my ears back in shame. He took a small leash out of his pocket and hooked it to my collar.

"I think we need to take you somewhere where you'll be safe, big guy. God knows you've suffered enough in this house.

It's time you had a little break."

When he saw my ball in the grass, he smiled again. "Is this yours?" He picked up the pink toy and handed it to me. I squeaked it a few times, then followed him to his car with the ball in my mouth.

As we pulled away from the burned ruins of what used to be my home, I realized that Tommy's blanket was the only valuable thing I left behind. Otherwise there were just memories—many of them not worth keeping. I couldn't help but wonder what lay ahead for me. Was Mike taking me to his house? Or was I going to the pound? Would anyone ever want me again? Or would I be killed, like Carlos warned? I had no say in any of it. It was the people in my life who decided where I lived, what I ate, when I drank, and if I lived or died. I guess that was all part of being a dog. Hopefully things would work out for the better. I was tired of being alone.

Chapter Eighteen

Clare

The man from heaven was nervous once again. In a way, he rejoiced to see the dog forced out of his disgraceful home. But he also feared where the cop would take him. From what he knew of the dog pound, it was a rough place and a lot of dogs were put to sleep. He would just have to watch and wait.

Meanwhile, he wondered about the dog's owner, Jim. He couldn't follow the unfortunate soul to its final destination. Wherever Jim went, it was a different sort of place—a place where unsettled spirits had to fix their troubles before they moved on.

This prompted the man to think of his wife. He knew she continued to anguish over a mistake he was trying hard to fix. After seeing what happened to Jim, he had to make sure the dog was safe before his wife died. If he screwed up and the dog was killed, the man may never see her again. He couldn't allow that to happen. And, knowing his wife's health wouldn't hold much longer, he didn't have a lot of time.

Byron

Our car ride was short. Before I knew it, we pulled into the parking lot of a large brick building surrounded by tall fences and trees. There was a sign on the front with pictures of dogs and cats. I figured we were at the pound.

"Okay, Byron, here we are. Don't be scared. My friend Tony is very nice, and I'm sure he'll take good care of you." Mike and I got out of the car, and he led me to the entrance of the building. From behind the walls, I heard a million dogs barking.

He opened the door and the noise was deafening. So many dogs barked and cried that my head swam and my ears hurt. Besides the barking, there were rattles, bangs, and clawing sounds that came from around the corner. I decided I wasn't going in.

"Come on Byron!" My friend had to yell as he tugged at the leash.

When I refused to budge, he got down on his knees and cupped my head in his hands.

"Okay, this is the deal, Byron. We're at the pound, and it's not a pleasant place. But, I promise it won't be as bad as it sounds. I think you'll like it better than your house. At least you'll have other dogs to talk to." He paused for a second and petted my head. "Tony is going to get in touch with the rest of your family to see if they can come get you. If not, I'm sure he'll find you a nice home."

He was so nice that I couldn't act stubborn anymore. Maybe he was right. I knew Marion wouldn't come get me, but there were tons of other people that might need a watchdog. Apparently that's what I was good for.

We turned the corner reluctantly and were hit with yelping that echoed so loudly, Mike had to cover one ear with his free hand. His face scrunched as we hurried past too many dogs to count. The room itself was large and gray, lined with crates halfway up to the ceiling. There were cages on the ground and cages that sat on cages. There were cages aligned in rows in the center, and crates stacked all along the walls. You couldn't stand in one spot without being surrounded by several of them. And, of course there was a dog in each one. Big dogs were on the bottom and little dogs on top. Not one crate was empty that I saw, and everyone barked.

The smell of the room reminded me of the putrid alley, but ten times worse. Not only was the air stale and hot, but there was no breeze or outdoor odor to cover up the dank stench that sat stagnant around us. We continued our walk and rounded the corner toward some offices.

"Hey Tony, how are ya, buddy?"

We entered a small room with a desk. Mike and Tony shook hands and patted each other on the back.

"Good, Mikey, my man, and you? Wow, look at the size of that shepherd. He's a beaut," said Tony, crouching down to look at my face. "I don't think we'll have a problem finding you a home."

"See, Byron, what did I tell you?" said my cop, smiling down at me.

"So, what was the deal with this dude Meloon?" asked Tony. "I only met him once, and he was a real jerk."

"Yeah, what a winner. I only met him a couple times myself, including last Christmas when his kid ran off with Byron here. The whole family was weird. I guess Meloon went berserk after Anderson was killed." Mike shook his head. "They found his remains up in a bedroom. From what I hear, his wife took off with the three kids a couple days ago and moved back to Kansas with her mother. No one knows anything else."

"Eh, what a shame," said Tony. "I feel bad for the kids."

"Me, too."

"Well, big guy, what do you say we find you a nice cage out there and get you some food and water? It's not the Ritz, but it'll have to do for now." Tony stood up and took my leash.

"Thanks, Tony," said Mike. "If he were less than twenty pounds I'd take him home with me. But you know those apartment people. I'd be evicted."

"No problem, dude. I'll make sure he's okay."

"Thanks, man. Oh, hey, I almost forgot." He pulled my ball out of his pocket and tossed it to Tony. "Make sure he hangs on to this. He had it with him at the fire."

The minute we stepped back around the corner, the noise started again. After spending the last year of my life in solitude, I knew I would have a hard time adjusting to the commotion. The headache that I got coming through the door hadn't resolved yet and it was bound to get worse.

Tony led me to a large cage against the back wall. The floor was cement, and it had a drain in the center. There was a fresh bowl of water and an old blanket for a bed. Tony gave me my ball and said he'd be back later to take me outside for a walk. He shut the door to my cage and I watched him walk away.

"What brings you here, Fancy Pants with the sissy ball?" The old gruff voice startled me as I turned to my right. A tall, brown boxer with drooling jowls and crusty eyes sat watching me from the cage next door. He stood up and walked toward me, limping badly on the left side.

"Did you say something?" I asked.

"Yeah, I asked you what brought you in," he said.

"My house burned down last night," I responded. I wasn't quite sure what else to say.

"Sorry to hear that. What happened to your family? Did they roast like toast?"

"Kind of," I said, thinking about Jim. "They didn't want me anyway."

"You and the rest of us, pal," chuckled the boxer. "My name's Joe Boxo. I've been here for three weeks. My time's almost up." He laughed.

"Hi Joe, I'm Byron." I was only half listening to him as I looked around me. I had never seen so many scraggly dogs. I thought the strays on the street were bad. But seeing this beat all. Besides Joe's crusty eyes, all of the dogs had dirty, matted fur with feces hanging from their bellies. Their faces were sad, and their eyes were dull. I was surprised they barked as loud as they did; they looked so tired and sick.

"I know what you're thinkin', German Boy, and it's all true. Just keep your chin up, and you'll be cool. We get some decent volunteers that walk us once in a while. The food's not too bad, and some of the chicks are cute. I just mind my own business and don't think about the bad stuff."

"What's the bad stuff?" I asked.

"You know, the Friday morning Kill List," he said casually.

"What?" I felt goosebumps on my neck.

"The Friday morning Kill List," he repeated. "What are you, a pound newbie? Every Friday morning some guys come around with a list of unlucky flea farms, and take 'em over to the doom room."

"What happens to them in the doom room?" I asked. I knew the pound was bad, but I wasn't sure why.

"They croak."

"They what?" I asked.

"They die."

"Oh," I said.

It was all too much information for me at the moment. Besides, I was so tired, I didn't know if I heard him right. I hadn't gotten any sleep since the day before and really needed a nap.

"Joe Boxo, it was nice talking to you, but I'm really tired and I've had a long night."

"Hey no problemo, Germo Shepo. Have a good snooze." He limped away, and I noticed his left hip was crooked. He turned his attention to a different neighbor.

I circled the concrete floor until I found the right spot. The rest of the dogs had quieted down, and I thought I might get a good rest. Just before I shut my eyes, I noticed the dog to my left. She had been quiet the entire time and pretended not to notice me. *Later,* I thought. *I'll meet her later.* I fell into a restless sleep.

Chapter Nineteen

Trudy

The old lady was failing fast. The last couple days had been especially hard on her, and she was told yesterday that she only had days to live. She wasn't sure if the nightmare two nights ago made her worse, or if it was just God's will. In a way she felt relieved. Her life consisted of no more than breathing and sleeping. She couldn't even eat; the effort was too great. But the real reason she welcomed death was because her mental struggle would end. The horrible images that came during her sleep would be gone for good. And at this point, there was nothing more she could do to fix her past. She had begged for God's mercy on her soul and the soul of the dog she had left behind. If her prayer hadn't been answered yet, she at least hoped she could make things right in the next life, if that one existed.

Late that morning, the woman swore she felt her husband's presence. A cool breeze swept past her face, followed by a warm caress on her bony hand. As she reached for him, the effort tired her, and she closed her eyes, hoping to join him that day. In a way, her wish was granted, but not in the form she wanted. As the woman fell into a deep sleep, another terrorizing nightmare took her back to a place she so dreaded. Desperately she tried to wake herself, knowing where she had slipped, but it was too late. She was already there.

Byron

No matter how tired I was, it wasn't enough to stop me from dreaming. My night had already been stressful, and I didn't know why I had to be plagued with such a horrible nightmare. I knew where my mind was headed the minute I closed my eyes. I fought to wake up, but it was too late.

Trudy and Clare sat in the formal dining room where the table sparkled with crisp linens and fine china. The evening sun shone through the clean glass windows, making prisms in the crystal goblets. Trudy was dressed in a lovely yellow dress, and Clare wore his gray pinstriped suit. They sat face to face across the table and couldn't have looked more picture-perfect. I wasn't in the room, but I saw and heard everything. Clare filled their glasses with champagne and prepared to make a toast.

He cleared his throat and smiled lovingly at his wife. "To my wonderful Trude," he began. "On our thirtieth wedding anniversary, I am still the luckiest man alive. I have three great kids, plenty of money, and the most beautiful wife on the planet. Here's to us, partner." He reached across the table and clinked glasses as he winked.

Trudy smiled back as small tears formed in the corners of her eyes. Looking down she giggled and said, "Oh Clare." After a moment she added, "Shall we pray?"

Together they bowed heads and said their dinner prayer of thanks, followed by a prayer for their deceased son in heaven. "...and may the souls of all the faithfully departed, through the mercy of God, rest in peace. Amen." They both cried silently, for that wound was still fresh in their hearts.

Dinner was served shortly after, starting with tossed vegetables from Trudy's garden and home-baked bread. Next, the main meal of turtle stew was served, which was Clare's favorite. Tonight he seemed to especially enjoy it. He chewed extra slowly and never stopped smiling.

"What was the surprise you had for me?" Trudy asked, after eating in silence for a while.

Clare took the pale yellow napkin off his lap and wiped his lips. He placed it back under the table and reached for his wine. "Well, honey, I put a deposit on a house in Bloomfield Hills tonight. That's why I was late." He sipped his wine, never looking at her face.

"Oh, I see." Trudy forced a smile and looked squarely at her husband. "That's very exciting, Clare. Tell me, when do you plan on moving us?"

Clare finally looked at her. "Well, I suppose if everything goes as planned, we could move at the beginning of October."

"But, that only gives us six weeks. How will we pack and move in such a short amount of time?" I could tell Trudy wasn't thrilled.

"If we need more time, I'm sure seven or eight weeks won't be a problem. With the maid's help, you'll be able to get it done by then."

Trudy patted her knees and stood suddenly with a big smile. "Well, Clare, since you had such a nice surprise for me, I have an even better surprise for you." A devilish grin lit up her face and made her lipstick dazzle even redder. "I prepared a special treat for you tonight."

As she talked, she bustled into the kitchen. "Since I knew we would have to give Thor up anyway, I thought I may as well kill him and bake his organs for dessert."

She came back through the doorway carrying a platter with my head on it. My ears were held up by toothpicks in the center, surrounded by baked liver crumpets and kidney cream cakes. Chocolate and vanilla marble ice cream scoops complimented the arrangement, dripping with cherries and hot fudge. My eyes were glazed over and cloudy, and my tongue hung lifeless on the platter with marshmallows on top. Blood dripped from the edge of the plate onto Trudy's hands, and she laughed watching it spill to the floor. Clare joined in the laughter and gave her a kiss in celebration.

I wasn't sure what to do and couldn't figure out where I really was. I knew I wasn't dead because I felt too alive. When I barked, about a hundred different voices came out of my mouth. Trudy and Clare's laughter blended in with the rest of the noise.

I opened my eyes and was momentarily confused until I realized I was at the pound. The barking came from all around, and the laughing was directly from the left. When I turned my head, I remembered my neighbor and decided it was a good time to make myself known.

Chapter Twenty

Byron

My neighbor was a medium-sized sheltie with big brown ears and a long nose. She had a sweeping upturned tail and white patches on her back. I thought she was pretty, except for the dirty mats and tangles in her long wavy fur. While she sat shyly, a young, pretty woman entertained her. The woman played peek-a-boo through her hands, smiling and laughing the entire time.

"Oops, I see Baby. Peek-a-boo, pretty Baby."

The two sat facing each other on the cement floor with barely enough room to move. I envied the dog who concentrated so heavily on the game. She didn't seem to notice the dozens of other dogs who barked and begged for the woman's attention.

"Are you ready to go for a walk now, Baby?" the woman asked sweetly to my neighbor. "It's a pretty day, and you need some sunshine."

As the woman stood slowly, Baby cowered and urinated on the floor. The woman got back down on her knees. "Oh, honey, I'm not going to hurt you. Maybe we'll try again next week."

After the woman gave her a kiss on the head, she noticed me staring at her. "Well, look who's awake. You must be... oh gosh, I forgot," she paused as she read something on the outside of my cage. "Byron. That's right. Tony told me about you. I'm Cindy, and I'm one of the volunteers. It sounds like you've had a rough couple of days."

I was so excited that Cindy talked to me. I wagged my tail and nosed the latch. She reminded me of Dora and as she opened the door, I jumped up and hit my head on the ceiling of the cage.

"Watch out, big guy. You're too tall to be jumping."

Joe Boxo got excited too. He started to bark.

"That's enough, Joe. No need to be that noisy," the girl scolded affectionately while pointing a finger. Joe listened and stopped barking.

She squeezed her body partially into my cage and stuck her hand out for me to sniff, but I opted to hug her instead. Jumping up, my paws easily touched her shoulders, and she almost lost her balance.

"Oh Byron honey, down! You're going to knock me over." She clung to the cage door, half laughing. "You are a moose, aren't you?"

I instantly loved her.

"I think you need some serious exercise," she said as she hooked a leash to my collar.

Outside, Cindy took me to one of the penned-in areas and let me off the leash. No one else played out there, which surprised me. It was a beautiful day, and the grass was nicer than my backyard. I ran around for a while, until Cindy took me back inside. When she opened the door, we were hit with another explosion of barking and pleading.

"Cindy, come see me!"

"Cindy, I want to go outside!"

"Cindy, I need to go potty!"

"Cindy, please play with me! I miss you!"

We headed toward my cage. As we passed some rooms off to the side, another woman motioned for Cindy to stop. Three tiny white puppies sat in a box next to her.

"Hi Joanie," said Cindy. "Oh my gosh, where did those adorable puppies come from?"

"Tony got a phone call last night from the McDonald's up on Norman Highway. Apparently, someone attempted to throw trash in the dumpster and was attacked by the mother. When Tony got there, he found the mom and babies back behind a bush. The mom's in quarantine right now, and I'm taking these guys to the vet. They look sick to me."

Cindy nodded sympathetically toward the puppies. "No wonder. Poor things. What kind of shape is the mother in?"

"Not good," replied the woman. "She's mean, and she looks mangy. I'm not sure we'll be able to socialize her. Tony had to use a tranquilizer to get her into the truck. She'll probably have to be put down."

"Well, I'll try and work with her before we go to that extreme. Let me know if I can help with the puppies," said Cindy, patting them on the heads.

"Thanks, kiddo."

Cindy and I continued to my cage. Every now and then, she slowed to put her hand to a dog and say hello. "I guess it's a good thing my mom won't let me bring any of you home," she said. "I'd have at least a hundred dogs by now." Cindy laughed, and we continued to walk.

"Okay, Moose Man, here we are." She unlatched my cage and patted my butt as I stepped in.

One more time, she looked at the sheltie, and said, "Bye-bye, Baby. I'll see you again next Thursday."

"If she's lucky to be alive," Joe mumbled under his breath.

"Hey, what about me, Cindy Loo Hoo?" he called.

"Bye, Byron. Bye, handsome Joe. See you big boys next week. I'll keep working on a home for you, Joe. We're almost there." Cindy walked away, and I heard everyone moan in disappointment. Cindy was like a bright shining star in a place where no one wanted to be.

Joe lay down, letting out a cry as he settled on his hip. "It's a shame she's always gotta go home," he sighed. "I think she was a koochie poochie in another life."

While he curled up in a sleeping position, I turned toward Baby. I was curious about her. She stood like a statue staring at the back of her cage and still wouldn't acknowledge me.

"Hi, my name's Byron," I said to her softly.

"I know," she said, still not moving her head.

"How long have you been here?" I asked.

"I'm not sure," she replied.

"She's only been here a week," interjected Joe from his fake sleep. "She's missing a few noodles, Germ Worm, so don't try to get in any deep conversations with her."

"What's wrong with her?" I said quietly as I turned back to face him.

"I think someone clocked her in the noggin one too many times." Joe shook his head sympathetically. "It's too bad, because, woo doggie, she's hot."

"How do you know this?" I asked.

"She sings about it in her sleep. And then when she wakes up, she has no clue. She's cuckoo, that's for sure. They'll probably do away with her before the usual time."

"What's the usual time?" I asked, not really wanting to know.

"One month tops," said Joe. "But Tony knows no one will adopt her. Every time someone looks at her, she whizzes like a walrus. The only person she'll talk to is Cindy."

"Why doesn't Cindy take her home?"

"Cindy can't take anyone home," said Joe. "She says her old lady won't let her. She's always spewin' some garbage about the old bag being allergic or something. It's all horse hockey to me." He paused. "Yep, Babes will probably bite the dust with me next week."

"With you?" My stomach suddenly turned in knots.

"My time's up, pup. I've been here three weeks already. Nobody wants a fat old Boxer with a bad hip. I should've bought the farm years ago when that truck hit me. Besides, I'm sick of livin' in this dump."

I didn't know what to say. Joe scared me with the things he talked about, and I didn't want to hear it. I tried having a conversation with Baby again, but she was in another world. As I watched her lie down to sleep, I couldn't help but feel sad. Baby didn't seem to know what was happening to her. Luckily Tony said I'd find a home, but what about the rest of the dogs? Now I understood why everyone avoided the pound, and why they were never seen again.

As I lay down on my own cement floor, I listened to Joe snore peacefully and Baby hum sweetly. Maybe they dreamed of better days and nice memories. Possibly their dreams would come true. I hoped that would happen someday for all of us.

Chapter Twenty-One

Cindy

Cindy loved dogs. She had volunteered at the pound since high school and wished she could do more. There were so many homeless animals, and every week at least ten dogs were put to death unnecessarily. It made her sick. If she could have taken home every dog that was going to be euthanized, she would have, but it was impossible. So she did everything else she could to make a difference.

Each week, Cindy got on the phone and called local rescues and shelters to see if any of them could take even one dog on the Kill List. Most weeks they were full and apologized that they couldn't help out. But once in a while Cindy got lucky, and a rescue would come through and pick up one or more dogs. On those days she felt great—like she had made a difference. But another Friday always followed, and more dogs were always killed. Cindy wasn't sure if her heart could take much more.

When Baby came along, Cindy had seen enough. Baby was so badly abused that she couldn't even be looked at without cowering. To take a dog like that and just murder her was more than Cindy could bear. She had fallen in love with Baby, and decided that if Baby was euthanized, she would quit volunteering.

Byron

Nothing much changed on a day-to-day basis. The only difference was the volunteers. My favorite was still Cindy, because she was the only one who took me outside. But it was fun to see them all. The only time there was nobody was on weekends. A policeman would stop in briefly and fill our water bowls, and that was it. No one got walked, and no one got fed. By Monday our cages were rancid, and we were starving. As much as I hated getting wet, I was always thankful for the person who hosed our floors down on Monday. Like Joe, I was tired of this dump.

Something really wonderful happened during my second week there. It was Thursday, and we patiently waited for Cindy to take each of us outside. I had avoided discussing Kill Day with Joe because I couldn't face the reality of it and didn't want to see him go to the doom room. As irritating as he was, with his crude jokes and talk of death, Joe was my friend. He knew everything and taught me a lot in the short time we were together.

As we lay discussing the day's events, we heard Cindy's voice around the corner and perked up.

"It's funny that you're looking for that breed, Mr. Foxtoe, because we have someone that you might be interested in." Cindy's voice was light and cheery.

"Ah, here we go again, another 'maybe' for Baby. When's that girly gonna learn?" Joe said as he rolled his eyes.

Baby was in la-la land as she sat in the corner, watching a fly climb over a pile of poop.

"Maybe it's not for Baby this time, Jo Bo," I said. "Maybe it's for you."

"That'll be a safe day in Detroit, Euro man; a day when your ears droop; a day when Baby-face doesn't cower; a day when—"

"Here he is, Mr. Foxtoe."

We all looked up, including Baby, and saw an older man limp in our direction. He followed slowly behind Cindy as she talked. He used a stick to walk, and his left hip was crooked.

Joe stared at the man as he approached our cages. The man smiled, and Joe's stub of a tail began to wag. I don't think Joe ever believed that anyone would want him.

"Well, look at you," the man said to Joe. "I've been looking for someone just like you. What is your name?" he asked.

"His name is Joe, Mr. Foxtoe," answered Cindy.

"Really. Isn't that something. My name's Joe also." The man laughed out loud and began to unlatch Joe's door. When Joe limped out from his cage, the man's face went from laughing to very serious. Cindy grabbed hold of Joe while the man collected himself and wiped his nose. He looked like he might cry. Just when Cindy was about to say something, Mr. Foxtoe turned back toward Joe and bent over. Tenderly, he said, "Well, buddy, not only do we have the same name, it looks like we have the same hip, too. I think we'll be perfect for each other."

Joe was so happy, he wagged his tail even harder until his hip almost gave out underneath him. Cindy's smile was the biggest I'd ever seen, and I was relieved. Joe Boxo wasn't gonna buy the farm after all. Joe Boxo was going home with

Joe Foxtoe, where they would live happily ever after. My friend didn't even turn to say goodbye as he limped proudly away and out of the dump forever.

"Wow, isn't that great, Baby?" I was so happy.

"What?" she asked.

"Never mind," I said, wishing she could share in the happiness.

Another week came and went, and still I sat. It was obvious that Marion wasn't coming to get me and no one else showed any interest. Several times a prospective owner walked past my cage, but when they saw me, they shook their head immediately. "Oh no, he's way too big." As much as I tried to make myself smaller and friendlier-looking, they always said no.

The Thursday after Joe left, Cindy took me outside to run. I was excited to be outside and took in every second of fresh air. A nice breeze blew over my ears and the sun felt good on my back. I could tell Cindy was sad. She looked distant.

"Oh, Byron, what are we going to do with you?" She finally snapped out of her trance, shading her eyes from the sun. "I've been working so hard on trying to find Baby a home that I haven't really spent time looking for you. I thought you'd be a no-brainer; you're so handsome."

I sat next to her feet, sniffing her pockets. They smelled like dog treats.

"Oh, do you smell a cookie, big boy? I almost forgot I had these."

Cindy stood up and took a Milk Bone out of her pocket. I hadn't had one since I lived at the warehouse. It tasted so good. When I was finished, she gave me a kiss on my head and said it was time to go in.

Back in the building, we passed by the same lady that had shown us the three puppies my first day.

"Oh hey, Cindy!" she called out.

"Hi Joanie, how are those puppies doing?" asked Cindy.

Joanie smiled. "I'm so happy. They all went to wonderful homes last weekend. It took about a week of antibiotics and good food, and they were set to go. We figured they were about six weeks old by then."

"I'm happy to hear that," said Cindy. "How about the mom? I haven't seen her yet."

"You know, Tony decided to have her euthanized tomorrow. She's still quarantined because she keeps attacking the staff. We can't risk anyone else getting hurt."

"Are you sure?" Cindy asked. "I could give it a shot." Her eyes filled with tears.

"What's wrong, honey?" Joanie asked. She put her arm around Cindy and petted my head at the same time.

"I don't know, Joanie. I'm just so tired of seeing all these dogs put to sleep. I wish there was more I could do."

"Oh sweetie, I don't think you realize how much you help them. Listen to all that noise. They love seeing you walk through the door. Look how happy Byron is now that you just took him outside. And Baby won't even look at anyone else. You do more than you think you do." Joanie was so nice. I loved her almost as much as I loved Cindy.

"Thanks Joan. I appreciate that. And, congratulations on the puppies."

She wiped her eyes as we walked back to my cage. I worried about her while she spent the rest of the day on the floor of Baby's cage. I saw the bond between them and wondered if I would ever have anyone in my life like that. All the things I ever wanted seemed so far out of my reach that I doubted they would happen. The big house, the huge yard, the loving family, the fun kids—it all seemed too good to be true.

That night I went to sleep feeling sorry for myself. It was the first time I had focused on my problems instead of someone else's. Joe wasn't there anymore to make me laugh and talking to Baby was like talking to a wall. As much as I tried not to get attached to her, it was difficult. She was so vulnerable, and I was protective by nature. I couldn't bear the thought of her being killed next week. Beyond that, what would happen to me? I was next. She had one week left, I had two. Cindy had admitted that she hadn't done much to help me, and I rarely saw Tony. He was the one who said I'd find a home. I began to doubt him.

In the morning, I felt sleepier than normal and was depressed from a night of sadness. Getting up to stretch, I didn't think my day could get any worse until I saw something dreadful. As I stared toward the main hallway through the pound, I saw a beautiful white dog being pulled in the direction of the doom room. As she was dragged across the floor, snarling, I realized who she was. She was the dog who ate from the dumpster the day I ran away. She was also the mother of the three puppies that Joanie had nursed to health.

My whole body went limp, and I fell to the floor in anguish. They were taking her to be euthanized, and there was nothing I could do about it. That dog hadn't done anything wrong. All she had tried to do this whole time was protect her children.

The look on her face was the same as Mama's the last day I saw her. She had done the best with what she had, and now someone was going to kill her for it.

For the rest of the day, I did nothing but sleep. I wouldn't even eat my dinner, knowing that I wouldn't have food for the next three days. Thinking about Baby getting dragged to the doom room next week was too much for me. Her time would come soon, and then it would be me.

Chapter Twenty-Two

Trudy

The old woman could barely breathe. As she lay in her hospital bed, she prayed that God would take her that night. The morphine didn't give her much relief, and her children stared over her like she was already gone. As many times as she said the Serenity Prayer, she couldn't accept her condition. Her past flashed painfully in front of her, while her future dragged incessantly behind her. She couldn't figure out which was what and began to talk nonsense as the nurse gave her more medicine.

While she prayed silently to herself, she noticed a priest standing over her. He was dressed in black with a look of empathy in his eyes. His hand gave the sign of the cross and his thumb blessed her forehead. To his left was her husband and to his right were her children, including the son who had died almost fifty years ago. How could that be, unless of course she was already dead? She dug her fingernails into her thigh, feeling pain that proved she was alive. Her eyes focused steadily on the priest, and his lips began to move.

"As Thor suffered to his death at the mercy of strangers, your soul will burn in the fires of hell throughout eternity."

The old woman panicked at his words and tried to scream, but could only squeak. She gazed toward her children to plead for help and noticed they were gone. When she looked at her husband, he was arguing with the priest. She would have loved to close her eyes, but was fixated on the strange image in front of her. What had she done to herself? Why had she made such poor decisions in the past? If only she could fix them now.

Byron

Luckily, Baby's last full day alive was a Thursday. Cindy came late, but at least she showed up. When I saw her, she had dark circles under her eyes and her face was puffy and red. She didn't even attempt to smile as she said good morning.

She stayed for only part of the day before she said she had to go. There was no mention of Baby's demise or a home for me anytime soon. Usually I looked to Cindy for hope, but today there was none, and Cindy didn't seem well. After she kissed Baby goodbye one last time, Tony came around the corner.

"Any luck with the rescues?" he asked.

"No," she responded bitterly.

"I'm sorry, Cindy, but you know we need the room, and—"

"Tony, you don't have to explain. I've been doing this long enough. I know the problems, the space issues, and everything else." She put her hands in the air as though to surrender. "I can't do this anymore." She started to cry. "This week it's Baby. Next week it's Byron. My heart can't take it. Five years of helping out, and I thought I could make a difference. I'm sorry, Tony."

She walked away sobbing, and that was the last I saw of

her. For the first time ever, Baby showed interest in what just happened.

"Where's Cindy going?" she asked me.

"I think she just went for a walk," I said.

"Oh."

That night I said a prayer. Joe had taught me one, and I thought it was a good time to try it.

"God (d-o-g spelled backwards), please don't let Baby die tomorrow, and please let me go home with a nice family. Amen (and may everyone nap)."

As weird as that was, I felt a little better and was able to shut my eyes. I should have known with all the stress of the day, I wouldn't sleep soundly. But what could I have done about it anyway? As my head hit the floor, I immediately went into a nightmare that I couldn't break away from. It was the worst one yet.

Trudy packed as I stood helpless in the driveway. It had been weeks since someone made the offer on our house. Now all my family had to do was move out, and the sale would be final. I hadn't met the new owners, but I was sure I wouldn't like them. The only person I wanted to be with was Trudy. And I knew she couldn't take me with her.

As she went about her business, she barely looked at me. Boxes were taped, and furniture was loaded on the truck, but not once did she tell me what would happen to me. Nothing had been packed from my doghouse, and my toys still lay all over the yard. I couldn't believe she would just leave me. I had never lived with anyone else and couldn't even remember where I was born. In my heart, Trudy was my only family, and I knew when she left me, nothing would matter.

Clare stepped outside to help with the last few items. The truck was loaded and waiting for the couple. All they had to do was get in their car and follow it to the city. Trudy hesitated with every step and looked like she would cry. I knew she loved me as much as I loved her.

Finally, the couple walked toward their car. Clare shooed me away repeatedly as I followed closely at Trudy's heels.

"Get in your doghouse, Thor. Get. Get!"

Trudy stepped in the passenger seat, never looking back or saying a word. I barked once, but was ignored as she shut the door. The car's engine started and they drove away. I sat alone in the driveway as the car disappeared down the dusty road.

Suddenly I awoke. The sadness of my dream was replaced with emptiness when I remembered that Baby was going to the doom room that day.

Chapter Twenty-Three

Clare

The man in heaven tried to think of a solution to the dog's dilemma. He knew he had a week before the dog was euthanized, but a week could go by quickly. The man had to work fast.

He thought about performing the radio trick again. But, honestly there was so much noise at the pound that no one would hear him. Plus there were too many dogs, and he couldn't be sure to get the right message across. He needed one person with a soft heart—someone who would take a dog like Byron into their home, at least temporarily. He had watched the little volunteer girl. But her mom wouldn't let her have a dog. Besides, she would no doubt take the sheltie before Byron. He needed to think of the right person. But who?

He tuned in to his wife for an idea or two. Although she wasn't in her right mind lately, she frequently cried about Thor and spewed nonsense about dogs in general. Today she had a visitor and babbled on about German shepherds. The man got a little closer to his wife's friend, and *bingo*! The man recognized her. She was the sweet young Polish woman who used to work for them in Bloomfield Hills. He remembered her name being Anna and that she quit her job in order to take care of stray dogs! The man had just found his perfect target. He eased quietly out of the room and began to think of a plan.

Byron

When they came to get Baby, I pretended not to notice at first. She didn't know what was about to happen, and I didn't have the heart to tell her. If Joe had been around, he would have found a way to make a joke. But I was glad he was gone. To me, there was nothing to joke about. Baby's life was about to end, and I couldn't do anything about it.

It was just before breakfast when two men came with a piece of paper and a long pole with a noose on the end. They laughed as they made fun of each other's wives and checked the name on Baby's cage.

"Yepper. This here's the one. Come on pooch, it's time for you to meet your maker and give up your cozy room to another mutt."

One man bent down to grab her while the other one bribed her with a cookie. "Come on, ya stubborn dog, we don't got all day now." The bent-over man reached his hand out to take her collar, and Baby backed up as far as she could go. Her tail slunk between her legs and her ears folded down in fear.

The man trying to catch her got impatient. "Ah, cripes. We had one like this last week. She wouldn't come out for nothin'. Let's go, poochie poochie." He tried to make his voice cute, but it just sounded obnoxious.

"Here, let me give it a try," the guy with the cookie said. He was almost too wide for the door, but he got down on his knees and crawled toward the back of the cage. As he tried to sweet-talk Baby, his partner stood outside whistling a stupid bird call.

Baby didn't buy it. The closer the man got, the more fearful she became. She began to growl as he cornered her.

"Now, now, little doggie. Don't get testy on me. I'm just a nice guy doin' my job. Me and Frank here aren't gonna hurt ya. We're gonna leave that up to the other guys." He laughed at his own bad joke, and so did Frank.

As Baby bared her teeth and warned them to go away, a stream of urine trickled down her back legs. Didn't that man realize what he was doing to her? I was sick to my stomach watching the whole thing. But nothing stopped him from trying. The more he coaxed, the louder she growled.

"If you don't get away from me, I'm going to bite your hand off," Baby muttered through her teeth.

I'd had enough and decided to help her out. I stood up and barked ferociously at the man. "Get away from her, you no-good loser! Back away, or she's going to bite you!" I yelled.

My sudden onset of barking startled both of them, and the guy on his knees bumped his head when he jumped.

"Goll dangat!" he screamed. He put his hand to his head and checked it for blood. "Frank, hand me that noose."

He took the long pole with the noose on it and began shoving it at Baby. Baby snarled and snapped at the pole while I barked and crashed my head against the cage bars. Eventually the rest of the dogs joined in until the whole pound was up in arms. Howls of anger, desperation, and disgust came from all over the room.

Unfortunately, Baby didn't handle things well. The more commotion there was, the more she panicked and the worse she got. Her body started to tire, and I knew she was about to give up.

"Baby, keep fighting him. You can do it!" I yelled at her. Her eyes darted from me to the man, and I could tell she was confused.

Finally he slipped the noose over her head and tightened it around her neck. As he pulled her toward him, she vomited and began to choke. I noticed blood trickling from her gums. Her claws dug into the concrete, but she wasn't strong enough to hold on. She slid closer and closer to the man and eventually collapsed.

Then suddenly out of nowhere, a voice yelled over the noise and the room went silent. "Hey! What are you idiots doing to that poor dog?"

Both men jumped, and the one on the floor dropped the pole. Baby scurried back to the corner of her cage while the men looked back at a tall woman staring angrily with her hands on her hips. She held a piece of paper in one hand and a leash in the other. I fell back with relief and noticed Baby breathing heavily on the floor with the noose still attached.

"Move out of my way." The woman spoke with a thick accent as she pushed herself through the cage door and removed the noose from Baby's neck. Baby was so tired by then, she didn't seem to care that the woman was near her.

"Who are you?" asked Frank, still wide-eyed.

The woman crouched by Baby, feeling around her neck and looking in her mouth as she talked. I was amazed as I watched her work. I'd never seen Baby so calm. "I'm Anna Leski from Companion Pet Rescue, and I'm here to take this dog home." She attached the leash to Baby's collar, then stuck the piece of paper in Frank's face.

"Well, all I know was that this dog was on the Kill List

for today," said Frank defensively. He pulled the list out of his pocket and looked at it. Anna yanked it out of his hand.

"This list is dated three days ago," she said. "It was changed early this morning after I spoke with Tony. Maybe if you did your job properly, things like this wouldn't happen."

"Hey, whatever, lady. We just do what we're told." The two men shrugged, then picked up the pole and walked away.

Anna got back down in front of Baby and spoke softly while petting her head, "Oh, you poor baby. Look at you, you're such a mess. I'm going to take you home and give you a nice bath. And then you can meet all my other puppies, okay?"

I was stunned when Baby's tail moved. It didn't move much, but it meant she was okay. When Anna stood up and gave Baby a gentle tug, Baby followed. It was like magic.

"Bye, Baby," I said.

"Bye, Byron," she answered.

Anna looked back as though she forgot something. Her eyes locked on mine momentarily and then down to the floor where my ball lay. For a second I felt a glimmer of hope tingle in my skin. But then she turned around and continued toward the door. My heart sank as I watched them disappear down the corridor. She and Baby were gone.

Chapter Twenty-Four

Anna

Anna was a dog rescuer. At forty-eight years old, she had spent one third of her life taking in homeless dogs and adopting them to loving families. She came from Poland with her husband in the late 1980s, with one dog, one child, and a medical background. While working with the elderly full-time, Anna began to save dogs off the street and soon realized her true calling. Before long, she started her own non-profit rescue organization and quit work all together. But because she had become so close with some of the people she worked for, she never lost touch with them. There was one older couple from Bloomfield Hills in particular. Anna grew to love them like grandparents and before long felt like part of their family. A few years ago the old man died, forcing his widowed wife to move in with their daughter. Then last year, the old woman became very sick and was told she didn't have long to live.

When Anna got a call that her friend was expected to die, she felt very sad and went to the house right away. Anna arrived to see her in a hospital bed comfortably staring out her bedroom window. A nurse was in the room, as well as the woman's granddaughter, who Anna regarded as a sister. The minute the old woman saw Anna, she began mumbling about German shepherds. Anna was glad she could listen to her friend and say goodbye one last time.

As she drove away sadly, her Polish radio station played

a mess of static. Through the noise Anna swore she heard a man's voice repeat the words "German shepherd" in English. *Weird,* she thought. When she reached for the dial, it stopped. As soon as she got home, the phone rang. It was a young girl from a local pound pleading for Anna to take an abused sheltie off the Kill List tomorrow. Anna told the girl she was sorry, but she already had too many dogs and wished her luck. Later that afternoon the face of a German shepherd kept flashing on Animal Planet between commercials. *Even weirder.* Anna wondered if she was hallucinating and checked her temperature. When the evening news came on, there was a feature story on the number of dogs a local pound put down every week. Oddly, it was the same pound the girl had called from earlier. And finally that night, as Anna slept, she dreamed of her dying friend's deceased husband who repeatedly pointed to a German shepherd with a bright pink object at his feet. She couldn't hear what the man said, but his face looked desperate. By then Anna was downright spooked and knew she had to do something.

The next morning, after trying to rationalize the previous day's strange events, Anna called the pound and told them to take the sheltie off the Kill List. Although she couldn't connect that dog with a German shepherd, there was a reason she had to do it. When she walked out of the pound that morning with the sheltie, she noticed the German shepherd with the pink ball. Her skin tingled with goosebumps, and she knew she had done the right thing.

Byron

It seemed like an eternity as I sat in my cage wondering what would happen to me. Baby had already left, I was sure of it, and I couldn't hear Anna's voice anymore. Dogs howled from all around, calling for the lady who had just rescued someone. I was devastated. I circled my cage a few times and decided to sleep my sadness away.

After I closed my eyes, the whole room lit up with excitement again. I felt the vibration of footsteps close by and figured it was the men coming for another dog. I couldn't bear to see anymore. But as the footsteps neared my cage, I looked out of curiosity. To my surprise, I noticed Anna walking toward me with a different leash in her hand. She pointed her finger and said, "I'm taking you, too. Come on."

What? Did she say she was taking me too? I wasn't sure that I heard her right, but my heart began to pound, and my tail wagged nervously as she unlatched my door. Before I knew it, she hooked me to the leash, grabbed my pink ball, and whisked me away. It happened so fast, I didn't have a chance to think. As we walked out the door into the sunshine, I realized my prayer had been answered.

"First stop, Catherine's Pet Parlor, you filthy mongrels." Anna smiled as the open windows ruffled our fur for the first time in weeks. I had never been so dirty. The back seat was lined with a white sheet, and when I moved I noticed gray stains underneath me. Dried clumps of feces stuck to our bodies and small black bugs jumped from me to Baby and back again. I hadn't noticed how itchy I was until that moment. And we stunk.

After a long drive, we pulled in front of a nice building and got out of the car. Through the window we saw dogs of all shapes and sizes being brushed and fluffed. When we walked in, a bell rang and everyone's heads turned. I felt so out of place amidst the clean, shiny dogs who held their heads high and proud. I lowered my own in shame and noticed Baby hiding behind Anna's legs.

"Hi, Anna, what can I do for you today?" asked a pretty woman with a cape over her shirt. She walked toward us, smiling. "Good grief, what hole did you drag these two out of?"

"Hi, Catherine. I know. They're stinky and gross. I just picked them up from the pound and was wondering if I could use a bathtub," said Anna.

"Of course, you can," she said. "I'll come back to help you in a minute."

"Thank you so much."

The noise in the place was loud, but in a good way. Big fans and small hand-held dryers blew everywhere, turning wet dogs dry and making them pretty. There were poodles with big red bows lining the walls and huge fluffy dogs lying on the floor. Mutts who should have been homely looked royal with their fancy haircuts and colorful collars. I'd never seen anything like it. Most of the dogs just stared curiously, but some were downright rude.

A Scottish terrier with a pink satin bow sat looking at herself in the mirror. When she saw our reflections pass by, she turned to face us. "News flash," she smirked. "You smell!"

"Be nice, Lucy!" scolded a big collie to her right. "They look traumatized."

"Yeah, that's just what they want you to think." Lucy went back to admiring herself, as a big box fan fluffed her shiny fur.

Catherine bathed me, and when it was over, I felt like a new dog. She cleaned my ears, clipped my nails, and gave me a purple bow. Baby looked beautiful also. She had a pink and yellow ribbon flowing down her long, silky neck. Anna looked proud as she walked us out.

"Well, aren't you a big handsome boy now, Byron. And, look at you, Baby. I hardly recognize you. I think you're ready to meet the rest of my dogs."

When we got to the car, Anna removed the sheet from the back seat and ushered us in. All the way home, our noses stuck out the windows smiling at the cars that passed us by.

Anna's home was so nice. We pulled into her driveway, and the first thing I noticed was how the garage attached to the house. *Good*, I thought. The closer the garage was to Anna, the more I'd see her. But when we got out of the car, we didn't even go near the garage. Instead we walked up to the front door of the house.

I hadn't been inside a house since Alice and Ben's. Even there, I was only allowed in the laundry room, kitchen, and porch. I stepped in the door cautiously, and my feet slid on the clean wood floors as we were bombarded with a herd of little dogs. They slid toward us and crashed into Anna's legs.

"Anna's home! Anna's home!" they cried.

"Hey, you guys, calm down. I brought someone here I want to meet." Anna got down on her knees to pet the little dogs. "This is Byron," she said touching my head. "And this is Baby," she said turning in Baby's direction. I towered over them, and they didn't seem to care.

"Yeah, yeah, hi, whatever." They barely even looked at us. "Come on, Anna. Come on, Anna. Come on, come on, come on," they repeated while running in circles around her legs. It was annoying.

She led us to a room in the back of the house where I met the rest of her dogs. One by one, we were introduced as she let us outside together. Everybody was friendly and welcomed me with slobbery snouts and wagging tails. There were two that I instantly bonded with. Alex was a kind and gentle German shepherd, and Wolfie was a collie mix who towered over me. Then there was Bonnie, Zorba, Sessie, Fluffy, Tramp, Watson, Poncho, and so on. I liked them all and wondered why they still lived with Anna.

"We're her foster dogs," they said in unison. Then Alex spoke alone. "Anna won't adopt us out unless she finds us the perfect families. Most of us go home with people who we love, but some of us have been here for years. Wolfie and I are too old to leave now."

I counted all the dogs and was amazed at how happy they seemed. I looked over at Anna, who studied Baby carefully. Anna had so much love in her eyes as she comforted my friend and showed her a quiet crate. It eased my mind to know that she was genuine and that she cared for every single dog in her house. Now I was one of them. I took a deep breath and relaxed. Living here wasn't my dream, but it was better than what would have happened. Anna saved my life.

That night when the sun went down, I was given my own big crate with a blanket to sleep on. To my right was Alex, and to my left was Wolfie. Underneath my chest was my ball.

Chapter Twenty-Four

There was no talk of death, and there was no doubt that I'd be cared for. Nobody cried in their sleep except Baby, and the only rattling of crates came from loud, vibrating snores. I knew I would be okay.

Chapter Twenty-Five

Trudy

The old lady took her last breath in the middle of a mid-autumn night. As free as she finally felt, her heart went out to her family who sadly mourned over her body. She gave them each a kiss on the head and went happily to her husband who waited by the light.

His face looked relieved as she joined his comforting spirit. She had waited so long for this moment and hadn't been sure if it would happen. The woman thanked God for His blessings and told her husband she had to check one thing before they moved on. She had to know what happened to Thor.

When she learned that her wish had been granted, she was thrilled. She was even happier to know of her husband's involvement. But what saddened the lady was discovering how Thor had suffered already in his short, new life. Why couldn't it have been easier for him? After all, he had done nothing to deserve the pain he endured. It was her responsibility, and she would have to fix it.

When she and her husband arrived at Anna's house, she watched Thor sleep and was overtaken with love and sadness. Although she was grateful for his safety, this wasn't the life she wanted for him. Memories of the past ran through her mind, and the woman reminisced of how it felt to be near him. If only she could move closer and touch him in his sleep. She remembered how good he smelled when she kissed his head.

Just once, she thought. *I want to touch him just once,* and then she'd leave him alone until God decided he should come back to her for the last time.

Carefully, as though someone might sense her presence, the woman knelt by Thor. She leaned over and gently wrapped her arms around his big warm body and kissed the top of his soft head. Lying over him, she felt his chest rise and fall as he breathed slowly and peacefully. His vibrant energy radiated through her soul, and she realized how badly she missed him.

"Oh, Thor. I'm so sorry, boy. I didn't mean for your life to be so hard, or I wouldn't have asked for you to come back. I love you, and I promise to make it okay."

A tear dripped from the corner of her eye and landed on Thor's long nose. His ears flickered and he stirred lightly.

"Come on, Trude, we better go," said Clare as she kissed Thor one last time.

Thor raised his head and briefly stared into her eyes. His sudden movement triggered the other dogs to awaken, and a flurry of barking took over as Trudy rushed out of sight. Although she felt bad for startling him, she knew he was okay.

As Trudy and Clare went back to check on the rest of their family, a thought came to mind. Trudy noticed her grand-daughter, Jenny, standing at her bedside and had an idea. Of course! Not only was Jenny Anna's best friend, but because of something Trudy had left in her will, Jenny could give Thor the perfect home. All she had to do was get Jenny over to Anna's. The rest was easy. Jenny would fall in love with Thor, Trudy's mistake would be fixed, and her job would be complete.

Byron

After being at Anna's for a while, I noticed how calm I had become. I went to bed tired and woke up rested. Food tasted better and I had more energy. The vet said my weight was stable and that I was as healthy as could be expected. There was nothing to fear, and I had no responsibilities. Although I had to share Anna with the other dogs, my ball and my memories were mine alone.

One night I was stretched on the lawn looking at the stars when Anna called us in for bed. The fresh air had tired me and I was ready for sleep. My belly was full and my thirst was quenched. That night like every night, there was nothing to do but relax. I had let my mind wander and remembered things that used to scare me. I thought back to my dreams and realized I hadn't had one since being at Anna's. I wondered if Trudy was out of my life for good.

As tired as I was, I couldn't sleep. Thinking about Trudy earlier had started something, and I had trouble getting her off my mind. All night long I awakened with sensations that she was close by. It was the first time in weeks that I felt restless. Whenever I focused on something else, she'd force her way back into my thoughts. Even as I slept she was on my mind. I swore she sat next to me and touched my face. I heard her say my name, and I smelled her perfume. She spoke so clearly that her breath tickled my ear. At one point a tear fell on my nose. After being paralyzed through most of the strange experience,

I was finally able to open my eyes. I saw her for a second, and then she was gone.

At that same moment, the other dogs began to bark. They must have seen her too.

"Who was that, Byron?"

"Where did she go?"

"Byron, who was that lady?"

Suddenly the light snapped on, and everybody looked at Anna, who stood puzzled in the doorway. She tied her robe and yawned. "What's going on in here? And, what's that perfume smell?"

She looked around until her gaze rested on me. She must have thought it was unusual that I was the only dog not standing or barking. "Byron, are you okay?" she asked as she walked toward my crate. She bent down and unlatched the door. After petting my nose, she lifted her fingers and looked puzzled. "Your nose is all wet. That's weird. Hmm." Then she whispered so no one else could hear, "Hey, would you like a cookie?"

I forgot about Trudy and followed her out to the kitchen. We went to the cookie jar, and she gave me a Milk Bone.

"You're fine," she said as I swallowed my treat. She wiped the water off my nose and walked me back to my crate. She kissed me goodnight then shut the door. "Okay, all of you go back to sleep and I'll see you in the morning."

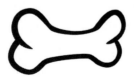

The next day, we had just finished eating breakfast when the phone rang. Anna spoke softly, then hung up. When she turned to face us she had tears in her eyes. I knew something was wrong and walked over to her. Everyone else followed. None of us were used to seeing Anna sad.

"Thanks, you guys," she said as she wiped her eyes and sniffled. "My friend died in the middle of the night, and I'm sad because she was such a good lady. I loved her very much." Anna cried quietly as more tears dripped down her cheek. "And she loved doggies, too, especially German shepherds, like you two." She put her hands on Alex's and my heads and ruffled our fur. Everyone else, feeling left out, pushed their way in. Noses poked from under her armpits, faces emerged between her knees, paws found their way to her shoulders, and little dogs jumped into her lap. After a couple minutes she giggled and shooed us away. "Okay, all you lovers, I better get ready because Jenny is coming over. She's sad about her grandma and needs warm fuzzies from you too."

Everyone got excited about the company and ran in circles. Nobody had visited Anna's house since I'd lived there, so I joined in the happiness.

"Yeah, Jenny's coming, Jenny's coming!" everyone yelled.

Anna straightened the house and swept the floors. She brushed a couple of small dogs and cleaned up the yard while we waited for Jenny to arrive. It was something new, and it reminded me of when I used to wait for Jim to come home. It was nice to feel excited and have butterflies in my stomach. I kind of missed that.

When Jenny walked in the door, I understood why everyone loved her. There wasn't one of us that she didn't pay attention to. When she looked at me for the first time, her face lit up, and I felt like I knew her.

"Oh, my gosh." She knelt down in front of me and held her hands firmly on my shoulders so I couldn't jump. Anna herded the rest of the dogs outside. Eventually I was the only one.

"Where did you come from, you beautiful dog?" she asked me, as tears ran down her cheeks. She seemed emotional, and I remembered that her grandma had just died. "Anna, where did you get him?"

"I haven't had a chance to tell you with everything going on. I got him from a pound the day after I last saw you and your grandma. I went to pick up a sheltie and ended up bringing Byron home, too. It's a long story."

"Oh my gosh, Byron, Grandma would have loved you," Jenny said, running her hands between my ears and down my back.

"I think your grandma is part of the reason he's here," Anna continued. "The timing was kind of weird, and it just seemed right. She was babbling about her shepherds just the day before, plus a bunch of other strange stuff happened."

Jenny was busy studying me and didn't seem to hear what Anna said. "You are huge, aren't you? Just a big moose."

Anna made coffee, and the two of them sat in the middle of the kitchen floor and talked. Jenny never once took her hand away from me. I was so relaxed as I rested my head on her lap, feeling the vibration of her voice and the warmth of her touch. It was only toward the end of their conversation that she mentioned me again.

"I can't believe this dog ended up at the pound. What's his story again?" Jenny asked.

"Didn't I tell you? I guess not," said Anna. She told her

about Jim and the house.

Jenny's face scrunched in disbelief. "I think I heard about that on the news. How awful."

"Luckily, Byron was outside and didn't get hurt. They found him wandering in the neighbor's yard the next morning, carrying a pink ball."

"Poor guy," said Jenny, as she cupped my face in her hands and kissed my nose. "Where's the wife and kids? Don't they want him?"

"No. The pound contacted her, and she didn't even know if Byron had been to a vet. She didn't know anything, except that he attacked her son and scarred him for life, which doesn't sound like Byron at all. She told them to put him down. Can you believe that?"

As much as it hurt me to hear it, I wasn't surprised.

"I don't understand people," said Jenny. "I couldn't even think to put Ruby down. Even if she did bite someone, there would have to be an explanation. Besides, she's part of the family. What's wrong with the world?" Then she looked at me. "You're such a sweet boy. How could anyone say you're mean?"

Who was Ruby? I suddenly felt jealous.

Anna spoke up. "Hey, maybe Ruby needs a friend. Maybe she needs a handsome mate like Byron to make her feel young again."

"No, she's too old. I think another dog would kill her. Besides, she's the queen and wouldn't appreciate having to share her kingdom." Jenny smiled and shook her head. "But, if I could have another dog, I'd take him. I've always wanted a German shepherd."

Jenny stopped talking suddenly and looked at Anna. "This

is really weird, Anna, but I wonder if my grandma sent me over here today to meet him."

"What do you mean?"

"Well, something happened after she died. Oh, never mind." Jenny lifted my head off her leg and kissed it. "Speaking of my grandma, I better go now and help my mom with funeral stuff. Thanks for making me feel better." Tears filled her eyes again as she stood to hug Anna. "I can't believe she's gone. I'm going to miss her so much."

"I know. She was a beautiful lady." Anna hugged her back.

I followed Jenny to the door. Something about her felt so right, and I didn't want her to go. As much as I loved Anna, there was a connection with Jenny that I couldn't explain. Before she walked out, she crouched down and looked into my eyes. "I would take you home in a heartbeat if I could. Whoever gets you is going to be the luckiest person in the world." She kissed me on the head one last time, and then she left.

Chapter Twenty-Six

Jenny

Jenny was an animal lover. She adored dogs and would have owned twenty if she could. But she worked and was married with two kids. She also had a twelve-year-old dog named Ruby, two parrots, and a cat. Her house was full, and her time was precious.

When she left Anna's house, something inside of her felt empty. Not only had she lost her grandmother that morning, but leaving Byron behind added to her sadness, and she couldn't explain why. Thinking back to a strange incident that occurred shortly after her grandma's death, Jenny wondered if old Trude had anything to do with the strong connection she felt with the dog.

It happened almost as soon as Jenny got to her grandma's bedside. She stood staring at the lifeless figure who had been such a strong influence in her life, and she suddenly became aware of someone's presence. First, a candle across the room flickered out. Then a cool breeze lifted the hair from her neck, followed by the feeling of a warm hand over hers that sent chills down her spine. Nobody else in the room seemed unnerved as they sat talking quietly. But Jenny knew that her grandma was next to her at that moment and wished she could reach out and touch her.

"Hi, Grandma," she whispered, glancing up at an old photo on the wall.

Another breeze, stronger than the first, went by and this time blew a piece of paper off the night stand. Jenny bent down to pick it up and noticed it was Anna's phone number. In her grandma's demented state, she had asked that the number be available in case she needed to find a home for Thor. *I'll have to call Anna*, thought Jenny at the time.

Driving away from Anna's house, Jenny pulled the piece of paper from her pocket. She studied her grandma's shaky hand-writing and smiled to herself. *Everything happens for a reason*, she thought. Feeling her grandma's strength, something inside of her began to change. Maybe having another dog wouldn't be so bad. It may even help Ruby, like Anna had said. After settling the argument in her head, she called her husband.

Byron

Later that day, the doorbell rang. Everyone went crazy, and Anna looked confused. "I'm not expecting anyone," she said to herself as she took us into the back room. "Go on now, and be quiet. Shush, you guys. Go on."

Her footsteps pattered back down the hall as she disappeared toward the front door. After what seemed like forever, she returned with someone following close behind. I couldn't tell who it was at first, and then Anna stepped aside.

"Cindy!" I barked. "Baby, look, it's Cindy!"

Baby was nowhere in sight. It was hard to see anything with everyone running in circles and knocking into each other. Cindy didn't even notice me, even though I made the biggest fuss of all. She was too busy scanning the room for someone else.

With a big smile and wide eyes, she pushed her way through the crowd of fur and slobber. Dogs jumped on her, licking her face and grabbing her legs. She stumbled a couple times, but stood strong against the stampede. When Cindy found who she was searching for, she began to cry and dropped her purse.

"Baby! Oh, my Baby, there you are!" She climbed over the last couple dogs that separated her from Baby. Her arms stretched in front of her, and she grabbed Baby around the neck and hugged her. Tears ran down her face and soaked Baby's fur. Baby peered at me from over her shoulder.

"Byron, why is Cindy here?"

"I think she's here to see you, Baby."

Cindy spotted me and cried even more. "Byron! Oh, I'm so happy to see you, too! Tony told me you were here." She reached over and scrunched my head.

Anna took Baby and me into the kitchen so she and Cindy could talk. The two women sat at the table while we lay at their feet. It was good to see Cindy again. She was one of the people I missed.

"So, tell me Cindy, you moved into your own apartment?" asked Anna.

"Yes, just a couple days ago. And they let us have dogs there, which is the best part about it. It's a little expensive, but I was able to pick up more hours at work since I left the pound."

Anna looked concerned. "What will you do with Baby while you're at work?"

Cindy smiled. "I work at a small vet clinic. She gets to go with me."

"That sounds perfect," said Anna with a smile. She looked down at Baby and me and winked. "You sure you don't want to take Byron, too? He takes care of her, you know."

"He always did," said Cindy. "He's a good boy, but I just don't have the room or the money to take two big dogs." She sighed. "I have a good feeling about Byron, though. I thought from the beginning he wouldn't have any trouble finding the perfect family, and I still believe that in my heart."

"I hope you're right, Cindy."

Anna stood to usher Cindy and Baby out of the house. For a second time that day, I walked someone to the door I didn't want to leave. As happy as I was for Baby, I was sad for myself. Nobody would ever fill her place in my heart.

"Bye, Baby. I'll miss you," I said.

"Bye, Byron. I'll miss you too," she responded.

I watched out the window as Cindy and Baby drove away and wondered when it would be my turn. As much as I accepted the fact that my dream wouldn't come true, deep down I still wished and waited.

Chapter Twenty-Seven

Trudy

Trudy was pleased with the way things went. Jenny had met Thor, and they connected just as planned. In fact, Jenny seemed resolved to keep Thor, and in a matter of days, Trudy's job would be done. She and Clare could finally enjoy eternal peace together.

It was strange how things worked out for the best. Never in Trudy's mind did she imagine Thor ending up with her family in some way. Although it may have been a painful journey for him, if everything went as expected, he would be in a better home than she ever dreamed. Whether she or Clare had anything to do with it wasn't the issue. Trudy knew in her heart that some things were meant to be. By the grace of God, Thor found Jenny, and that's all that mattered. The best part was still yet to come. All along, God had listened to her prayers with more care and forethought than she expected.

Byron

I couldn't stop thinking about Jenny. Whenever Anna mentioned her name, I got excited. I longed to hear her voice again and feel her hands on my back. I loved the fuss she made over me and hoped that she would change her mind about taking me home. But it had been days since I saw her, and there was no mention of her coming over soon. Her grandmother's funeral had come and gone, and for sure she felt better. Anna did, I could tell. She was back to her old self, smiling and singing songs while she cooked. If Jenny was anything like Anna, she was okay, and I probably wouldn't see her for a while.

Baby was also doing well, I assumed. Several times I overheard Anna on the phone, saying stuff like, "Oh, Cindy, I'm so glad it's working out," and "Baby is so lucky to have you." Things turned out well for everyone, I guessed. Life was good, and I had nothing to complain about.

One afternoon while I napped on the porch, Anna hung up the phone and danced in from the kitchen. I hadn't heard the conversation, but I could see how excited she was. She shimmied toward me with her arms outstretched. "Goody, Byron, we did it!"

I jumped up to hug her. She put my paws on her shoulders and turned me in circles. She began to sing in Polish, then kissed me on the cheek.

"I have a surprise for you, big boy, and I know you're going to love it!"

Anna was like a little kid when she got excited, and that's what I loved so much about her. I wondered who she just hung up with.

She fluffed my ears a little and picked loose hair out of my coat. She checked my paws and felt my nails. "Okay, big guy, I guess we're good to go. Get your ball, and I'll find your leash."

I was confused.

"Go on, Byron. Go get your ball." She bent over and pointed to my crate while pushing me in that direction. "We're going for a ride."

It took me a few seconds to register that she was taking me out of the house. I dashed happily out to the dog room and grabbed my ball. When I got back to Anna, she held a leash in one hand and her purse in the other.

"Are you ready, big boy?" she asked as she attached the leash to my collar.

Of course I was. My tail wagged ferociously, and I bolted to the side door, forgetting my ball.

"Wooo, wait a minute. You're going to pull my arm off." Anna ran behind me, laughing. She held open the door while we stepped into the cool breezy afternoon. Once in the driveway, we got in the car and drove away.

After a fairly long drive, we turned onto a street of nice houses and huge trees. The leaves had turned orange and red and formed a colorful tunnel over the road. It felt good with the windows open to the fresh fall air as we drove through the pretty neighborhood.

We pulled into one of the driveways and Anna turned off the engine. Birds sang from up in the trees, and children laughed in the distance. The smell of burning wood filled my nostrils as chimneys puffed smoke into the air. Dogs barked from all around, and I could still hear the whir of traffic from the busy road we just came from.

Anna let me out of the car while I studied the house. It was pretty red brick with a big front porch and white pillars. The garage was attached, and a short white fence outlined where the backyard started. Pots of big red flowers sat by the front door. Through the picture window, I saw a fluffy white dog sleeping in a chair. She didn't seem to notice us as we walked up the brick drive and toward the front door. Once there, a tall, dark-haired man passed by the dog, waving as he came to the door. Anna didn't have to knock, and the dog didn't budge. The door opened and the man smiled.

"Hi, Anna. Come in, you two."

"Hi Larry," Anna replied.

Larry got down on one knee and let me sniff his hand. "You must be Byron."

Anna let go of my leash. I wagged my tail and licked the man's face. Something about him smelled familiar.

Then I remembered the white dog and walked over to her. She was the same breed as the one from the dumpster, but prettier and older. The minute I got close, she woke up and jumped down. We walked in circles as we sniffed each other and introduced ourselves.

"I'm Byron," I said, excited to meet her.

"I live here," she replied, not so happy. As she passed in front of me, she tripped on the wood floor and almost lost her footing. "Oh!" she cried.

"Byron, come!" called Anna.

I was suddenly embarrassed and hoped I hadn't caused her to get hurt. I walked quickly back to Anna.

"You have to be careful of Ruby. She's old, and you're big," she said gently, as she took hold of my collar again.

Ruby? I had heard that name before. And the smell of the

man—where was I? Then it hit me. Jenny! Ruby was Jenny's dog, and the man's clothes smelled like Jenny! At that same moment, I heard footsteps banging up a stairway in another part of the house. I pulled away from Anna, yanking the leash out of her hand, and ran toward the noise. The minute I rounded the first corner, I saw her. She carried a basket full of laundry and dropped it the instant she saw me.

"Byron!" she yelled happily, as I ran over to her and jumped onto her shoulders. "Oh my goodness, I missed you. I didn't hear you sneak in, you big moose." She kissed me on the nose as I wagged my tail and stood on my hind legs. We were the same height.

"Jake! Josie! Come see who's here!" Jenny yelled. She put my paws back to the floor.

More footsteps pounded around the corner, along with Anna who peeked in with Larry to watch us.

"Oh, hi Anna," laughed Jenny. "Kids, come here and meet Byron."

Two children, older than the Meloon boys, ran up to me and immediately got down on their knees. The boy was older and reminded me of Tommy. The girl was smaller, and I could tell that my size didn't bother her. Both of them rolled onto the floor and started to wrestle with me. Surprisingly, the adults didn't care. They seemed to like it!

"Look at them play," said Larry. "It's as if they grew up together."

"Yep, I think Byron is going to be happy with his new family," said Anna, looking pleased.

When I heard her say the words "new family," I felt a twinge of anxiety. Anna was giving me up? But, before I knew it, the kids distracted me again. Then Larry got down on the floor and rolled around with us. It didn't seem real. The kids played, the grown-ups played, and I played. How could so many people be happy and nice at the same time? Nothing felt bad, nobody yelled, and everyone was safe. It was like the dream that hadn't yet turned sour.

Eventually, the kids took me outside and showed me their backyard. Ruby came out for a second, but I knocked her over accidentally. I felt bad, but no one looked angry. Then Jake showed me his bedroom and I loved it. It was everything I imagined, with blue walls, baseballs, and clothes everywhere! I was even allowed on his bed. Josie's bedroom was great, too. There were pictures of horses on her walls and a mouse named Minnie in the corner.

Little by little I got used to Jenny's home. It was only the third house I had been in, and it was my favorite so far. The den had two big cages with birds in them, and the basement had a litter box. Unfortunately, the owner of the box was nowhere to be found.

"Jackie Sassy Cat must be hiding," mentioned Jake, as he searched around.

When we went back up to Jake's room to check under his bed, I heard Anna's keys rattle. I ran quickly to the living room and saw her gather up her purse.

"Okay Byron, I have to go now," said Anna sweetly. "You be good for your new family, and I'll see you soon."

Something was wrong. She was leaving without me. I ran

to her side, but Jenny grabbed my collar.

"No, no, Byron. You get to stay with us tonight," she said, trying to be sweet.

"Anna, wait!" I yelled, but it came out as a cry. Anna waved as Larry closed the door behind her.

Jenny held on to my collar as we all watched Anna walk out to the car—our car—the car we both came in and the car we should both leave in. As the headlights turned on and Anna backed out of the driveway, I was devastated.

And then I remembered my ball. I had left it at Anna's house.

"Anna, come back! Anna, please come back!" I was desperate, more than I had ever been before. I began to cry loudly and ran in circles around the house trying to escape.

"Byron, what's wrong?" Jenny came toward me and placed her hand on my head.

How could I explain that the only person I ever trusted just left without me? I didn't even have my ball. As much as I liked Jenny, I felt scared and alone. I pulled away and ran back to the front window looking frantically for Anna's car. Facing the street, I jumped on the large pane of glass, feeling it bow at the force of my paws. When I landed, my balance wavered and I crashed into Ruby's chair. She woke up from the jolt and barked.

"What in the world?" she asked, glancing around the room.

In my peripheral vision, I saw Jenny reach for me as I circled to jump again. "Byron, NO!" she yelled, yanking my collar. Her firm tone startled me, and suddenly I felt trapped. I began to panic and, thinking back to Tommy, was afraid I might hurt her.

Larry stepped forward. "Jen, be careful. We don't know him that well yet."

"Mom, what's wrong with Byron?" asked both kids, as they came into the room.

"I'm not sure, but just leave him alone until he settles down," she told them.

Jenny let go of my collar, and I rushed to the back door. I knew there was no way out of the yard, but the white fence was shorter than the Meloon's, and I had cleared that easily. I waited for Jenny to open the door and then rushed outside to the fence. After eyeballing its height one more time, I ran to the back of the yard. I stood for a moment, preparing myself mentally for the challenge. With all my might and all my energy, I charged toward the obstacle. Approaching it at lightning speed, I pushed myself off the ground and launched high into the air.

"Byron, no!" Jenny screamed, as I reached the soft grass on the other side. But I continued to run, crossing the front yard and heading in the same direction as Anna's car. Behind me a door slammed, and footsteps smacked against the sidewalk in my direction. I didn't look back because I knew I was faster than any one person. Seconds later I heard a car start, followed by the hum of an engine close behind. Cutting through several yards, I was able to escape my captors but was confused momentarily about where to go. When the traffic noises got louder, I knew I was headed the right way. Anna had called the busy road Woodward Avenue, and as long as I followed it, I knew I could get home. When the gas fumes got stronger, I figured I was close. Then when I rounded the next corner, engine noises exploded around me, and I was face to face with the highway.

Headlights followed headlights, and trucks revved and roared. Hot swooshes of air and loud bursts from tail pipes surrounded me, as several cars at a time blew past at high speeds. Just ahead was a stoplight with signals that told you when it was safe to cross, but I didn't know what they meant, and I didn't have time to find out. I had to get home to Anna.

At that moment Jenny screamed my name again. Quickly, I looked to see her running toward me. I turned my eyes back to Woodward and continued in that direction. I didn't know what to do and had become disoriented and dizzied by the lights. Jenny had almost caught up.

"Byron, COME!" she screamed. "STOP! Byron, STOP!"

But, I didn't. I took my chances and crossed the road.

Chapter Twenty-Eight

Trudy

Trudy watched in horror as Thor was hit by the car. As much as she tried to stop it from happening, she was powerless. All she could do was call out his name, which translated into a small gust of wind, unnoticeable among the roaring traffic.

She was even more disturbed seeing Jenny's reaction. Her granddaughter stood at the corner screaming and crying. She flailed her small arms desperately trying to stop the flow of cars, but not until two of them collided did traffic finally halt. By then, it was too late. Jenny's eyes caught sight of Thor's body lying in the middle of the road. Trudy knew her granddaughter fell apart inside as she ran to help him. She also knew that guilt would overcome her as it did to Trudy years ago. Things had gone so well until that moment. Now if Thor died, it would all end. He would never get his second chance, and Trudy would perish in hell. The only thing she could do at that moment was pray. It had worked when she was alive. Maybe it would work even better now that she was dead.

But as she begged for help one last time, her beautiful dog stopped breathing. Everything that mattered was no longer relevant as he lay lifeless in Jenny's arms. The feeling that pained her before she died came back. And as it did, Clare's spirit slowly faded. Trudy was left alone to mourn.

Byron

Throughout my life, I had many opportunities to contemplate death. It seemed like I was always on the fringe. Just one more step, one more day, or one more unlucky moment, and it could be my last. Both in my dreams and in day-to-day events, I looked at life as a temporary thing. I wished for people and places that I knew would never exist. I even thought that dying might be easier than living. I was tired of trusting people, and I didn't want to live on the street for the rest of my days. I was alone and confused, and like any dog, wanted that one person who would love me until death do us part.

Trudy was who I thought of as I lay sprawled out and bleeding in the middle of the highway. I wasn't sure why; maybe because she had been the only consistent person in my life. Or maybe because I was desperate, and my dreams were the only things I really had. Even the gawkers who came to stare reminded me of her. I couldn't shake the feeling that she was with me.

"Don't touch him," someone said.

"Yeah, animals are unpredictable when they're hurt," said someone else.

"Byron!" came a scream from beyond the small group. "Oh, my God, move—that's my dog! Byron, oh my God! Byron!" The small crowd parted, and Jenny pushed her way to my side. Besides the sirens in the distance, the air was eerily quiet, and everything moved in slow motion.

Jenny leaned over me and stroked my head. Her tears fell on my face as she rocked back and forth sobbing. I could barely feel the touch of her hands on my body. When I looked in front of me, my legs were tangled and didn't seem attached. My head felt warm and wet, and Jenny's voice echoed in my ears. It hurt to breathe.

"It's okay, boy, it's okay. Larry's coming with the car, and we're going to take you to the vet. You're going to be okay. Please, God, please. Oh, Byron, I'm so sorry. Please, God, make him okay. It was all my fault." She cried harder as she held my head firmly in her hands. A man's voice interrupted the sound of her sobs.

And that was the last thing I remembered.

Trudy waited for me. Her face followed my movements as she stood in front of the light. I happily made my way toward her, and she touched me with her feather-like fingers. I put my head against her body and felt her warmth. My soul melted into hers just like I remembered, and we intertwined in a way that was hard to describe. I had missed her so much and couldn't believe we were really together. We were alone in a world of nothingness, just me and Trudy, the way it was supposed to be—the way I had always dreamed. I loved her so much.

Trudy spoke softly as she caressed my cheek. "Thor, honey, you don't belong here right now." Her voice was smooth and clear. "I've missed you so much over the years, but this isn't how I wanted your life to end. There's still so much I want for you—so many things I didn't give you."

She was so sweet, and there was a confidence in her voice that told me I should understand her, but I didn't. She got down on her knees and stared into my eyes.

"When I left you at our home in the country, I tried to tell myself it was okay—that you belonged on a farm and not in the city. I didn't know it would turn out the way it did; that you would die alone in your doghouse." She paused. A tear formed in her eye and disappeared as it touched her cheek. "Years later, when I found out that you had frozen to death, I was sick. You were my dog, and I let someone do that to you, Thor. I let someone neglect you. I should have known, and I was wrong. I suffered the rest of my life knowing that. You were only six years old, and you were my dog."

Her head bowed toward her feet. I thought she had fallen asleep, she sat for so long. The silence gave me a moment to absorb what she said. When she spoke again her words came quicker.

"I tried to make it up in ways that didn't matter. I gave more money to charities and volunteered more of my time at church. I thought those things would ease my mind, but nothing worked. I thought about you every day and every night. Whenever something good happened in my life, I couldn't enjoy it, knowing how you must have suffered."

She shook her head and wiped away another invisible tear.

"Only once did I discuss my feelings with Clare, but he thought I was ridiculous, so I never spoke of you again. Then after he died, I started to panic. I knew my time would come to an end sooner than later, and I was afraid of going to hell and never seeing Clare or my son again. I wanted to make things right in my life, and I couldn't change what I had already done. So I prayed. I prayed that God would put you back on Earth and give you a good home with people who would love you forever. I prayed that you would have a second chance at happiness and that you would never have to worry about anything again.

"But, the more I prayed, the worse it got. I began having horrible nightmares that I maimed and killed you. The dreams got so bad that I could hardly sleep anymore, and I figured God was punishing me. As much as my daughter and granddaughter assured me I was a good person, I didn't believe them.

"The night I died, Clare took me to you, and I was so relieved. He had helped you the whole time. He kept you safe and eventually got you to Anna's. Even though in his lifetime he wasn't much of a dog person, Clare was always a good man. He knew I suffered from guilt and didn't want to see either one of us get hurt. He heard my prayers and worked as your angel."

Trudy took my face in her hands and looked at me closely. She spoke as though her words meant everything.

"You were not supposed to get hit by a car, Thor. My beautiful dog, dying this early wasn't in the plan. You have to go back to that family and let them love you. You can trust them, and I promise you won't be disappointed. We'll have our time together someday, but for now you have a long, wonderful life to live."

Suddenly, Trudy looked back toward the light and her face lit up. A male form stood in the distance, holding out his hand to her.

"It's time to go, Trude," he stated confidently. "These last few moments were a gift. Now you can both be at peace and enjoy what lies ahead. Byron, go to your new family. Trudy, come with me. Our son is waiting."

Trudy kissed my head and turned to leave. As I watched them disappear, I thought about everything she had just said, and it all made sense. She called me Thor because I was Thor in a different life. The nightmares I experienced were fragments of hers, created by her overwhelming sense of guilt. Dreaming together was a result of our deep connection and ancient love for one another.

I stood alone, but I wasn't afraid. I was ready to get back to Jenny. If Trudy said I could trust her, then I knew everything would be okay and I could start my new life.

I wished Trudy could go back with me, but I understood why that was impossible. She had only been real for that short moment; long enough for us both to mend our hearts and move on. Although I knew she'd always be with me in spirit, I wouldn't see her again like that for a very long time.

Chapter Twenty-Nine

Byron

When I woke up, I felt every bone, muscle, and twinge of pain in my body. I also saw five faces staring at me. Jenny, Larry, Jake, Josie, and Anna smiled as I opened my eyes. Jenny took in a deep sigh and began to cry. Next to me, peeking out from my blanket, was my ball. I couldn't have felt more loved.

I stayed at the vet for several days before my new family took me home. There was a hard cast on one leg and a bandage around my head. I couldn't move very well because of all the pain I felt, especially in my chest. The vet told Jenny that it might take months before I was back to my old self. Personally, I didn't want to be my "old self" ever again. I was a new dog with a new life, and that's the way I wanted it to stay. Trudy was right when she told me I would be happy. The only thing I didn't have was acres of land overflowing with deer and wild turkeys. But that was okay. I was so grateful for everything else, I figured I could wait until my next life.

Going home was an experience. When we pulled into the driveway, I noticed that the short white fence had been replaced with a very tall wooden one. Inside the house, Ruby greeted me with a little more enthusiasm.

"Hi, Byron. I'm glad you're okay," she said, looking at the floor.

"Thanks, Ruby," I responded. "Maybe you can show me how to do things better."

Ruby laughed. "I'll try. The only things they really don't like are muddy paws."

"Hey, big Byron boy, come look in my room!" yelled Jake.

I limped behind him. Thinking I would finally see our invisible cat, I saw something even better. There on the floor was a big thick blanket laid out for me. He took my ball out of his pocket and set it down. His bed was a tail's length away.

"You can sleep on this until you feel better. And then you can sleep in bed with me," he said, bouncing on his mattress.

"No, he can sleep with me," interrupted Josie from the hallway.

"Hey, maybe I want him to sleep with me!" yelled Jenny from the kitchen.

"No fair, Mom, he's my dog," said Jake.

"No, mine," said Josie.

"Don't worry, buddy, you can be mine," chuckled Larry, as he walked by and patted my butt.

"Oh well, I guess no one wants me anymore," said Ruby, lumbering through the kitchen and into Jenny's arms.

"Hi, my beautiful Roobs. How's my best girl today?" Jenny squeezed Ruby and kissed her a bunch of times on the face.

"Hi girl," said Larry, as he bent down and gave Ruby a long noisy smooch.

"Hey, Roobs," said Jake, poking his head out of his doorway.

"Ruby doobie doo!" yelled Josie, running up to her and smothering Ruby with a hug.

"Yeah, I guess nobody wants you," I replied as I limped over to them.

Ruby's tail wagged, and she turned away proudly. "Come on, Byron. I'll show you where the Milk Bones are."

For the next couple months, I continued to feel better. Eventually my cast was cut off and I walked normally again. Chasing Jackie became my favorite pastime, and soon enough Jenny bought me my own crate. I had become an equal part of the family.

As the weather turned colder and the trees lost their color, snow fell from the sky and Christmas sneaked up. Thankfully, it was different this year. I was in a warm house with my family who loved me. There was even a Christmas present with my name on it under the tree.

When Christmas Day came, the excitement at our house was overwhelming. The kids woke up early and barged into our room to get Jenny and Larry out of bed. Once downstairs and around the tree, wrapping paper flew and toys lay scattered everywhere. Ruby and I each got a new stuffed animal, and we both opened a large bone wrapped in Christmas paper. It was fun.

That afternoon, we had to get ready for our company. Jenny's parents were about to arrive for Christmas dinner and more presents. While holiday music blared from the stereo, Jake and Josie cleaned up their rooms, Jenny cooked dinner, and Larry straightened the house. Ruby and I lay by the fireplace and mouthed our toys. Over in the corner, the tree branches rustled.

"Jackie, get out of the tree!" Larry yelled suddenly, as a glass ornament smashed on the wood floor.

Jackie took off running across the room. I dropped my

stuffed animal and chased her through the dining area, scattering the broken glass as I slipped and slid around the corner. The birds screamed from the den, and Larry ran after me. "No, Byron! No chasing the cat!"

"Byron, you naughty boy, stop chasing poor Jackie or I'll have to put you in your crate," said Jenny, as she pulled something wonderful out of the oven. "Okay, you guys, hurry up. Nonnie and Papa will be here any minute!" She clapped her hands with the oven mitts and stood looking at the tree. I listened as she said sadly to Larry, "I can't believe this is my first Christmas without my grandma. It's not going to be the same."

"Well, let's just look at it as the first of a new tradition," said Larry positively. "Byron can take her place this year. Just think, someday, we'll be the grandparents."

"Yeah, well, I'd rather not think," Jenny laughed.

As Larry swept up the last of the broken glass, the doorbell rang. Ruby and I went to greet our guests, who came in carrying a big stack of presents.

"Merry Christmas, everyone!" they yelled. They stomped their feet and sent a dusting of snow across the floor. Jenny hugged her parents at the door, while the kids ran up and stood next to Ruby and me. "Hi, kids. Hi, Ruby, you sweet girl. Hi, Larry."

"Merry Christmas, John and Julie," said Larry, taking their coats.

Julie—I'd heard that name.

She turned to me next. "And you must be Byron. Oh, look at you, you gorgeous moose of a dog." She stared up at her daughter with wonder in her eyes. "Oh, honey, would Grandma have loved him. Wow."

I hadn't met Jenny's parents before, but I instantly loved them. There was something about her mom that I couldn't put my paw on. It was like when I first met Jenny. I wanted to be near her, and I felt strangely protective.

When the family sat down to eat, Larry asked Jenny's dad, "John, would you please say grace?"

Our family didn't usually pray before dinner, but tonight we did. It must have been a tradition with Jenny's parents, because John nodded.

"I'd be honored." He bowed his head and prayed. Afterward, Julie added, "...and may the souls of all the faithfully departed, through the mercy of God, rest in peace. Amen."

John added, "Merry Christmas to anyone who's watching us from heaven." He looked up and raised his glass. Everyone joined in.

"Hear, hear!" cheered Larry.

After dinner, we gathered around the tree to open presents. I stayed close to Julie, warming her feet and enjoying the feel of her hand on my back. The kids opened their gifts first. Then, Julie announced that she had a special surprise for Jenny and Larry. My two owners looked at each other and shrugged.

Julie pulled a piece of paper from her purse and placed her glasses on her face. She looked directly at her daughter and began to speak.

"I have saved this gift since your grandma died. Although it was in her will, she wanted me to wait until Christmas. You know Grandma. She loved the holidays, and she wanted this to be your present."

Julie unfolded the piece of paper and read aloud.

"To my granddaughter, Jenny, I have left a special something for you and your family. It was part of my life many years ago when I was your age. I raised my children with it and then regretted having to give it up. Last year it became available again for purchase, and something told me that my money would be better invested in that than sitting in slow-growing accounts. Also, knowing you and Larry, and your love for animals and the outdoors, I felt that you might be happier living in a place where your family can grow, run, and play."

Julie paused. She removed her glasses to wipe a tear, then placed them back on her nose. Jenny looked at her mother perplexed, and Larry stared at Jenny with a funny look on his face. The room was silent except for the crackle of the fireplace.

Julie sipped her drink and continued, "And so, after much thought, I bought you the house in the country where your grandpa and I raised our family. I also purchased the property that went with it. We had many wonderful years there, and I hope you love it as much as we did. I also hope your children collect many beautiful memories like your mother did, as well as dogs, cats, horses, and chickens. After all, those are the things that will fill your home with joy and keep you believing in love."

I looked at Jenny and Larry as they stood with their mouths open. After a few moments, Jenny smiled, and Larry shook his head in disbelief. Jenny walked over to Julie and hugged her for a very long time. John stood up to shake Larry's hand.

"Trudy never ceases to amaze me," he said, chuckling. "She was quite a woman."

"Unbelievable," was all Larry said.

Then I understood. I understood everything.

Chapter Thirty

Byron

The late afternoon sun shone through puffs of fair weather clouds as it warmed my fur. Leaves from above shimmered a bright mix of reds, oranges, and golds while those on the ground tossed about playfully. I sat stretched out on a freshly cut carpet of grass staring at my reflection in the pond. My head was mostly black except for some tan that ran from my eyebrows down to the tip of my nose. My ears stood perky and sharp. My neck was light tan as well as my legs, and I had a coal-black coat on my back and tail. I looked across the water to thick fields and dense forest, hearing bullfrogs croak among the reeds. When I turned my head toward the road, my house sat proudly overlooking our land. It was a two-story, white wood-sided farmhouse with lots of windows. A brick chimney jutted out from the green shingled roof curling smoke into the air. I called it my castle. I felt happy and content. My stomach was full, and I was loved.

Jenny, my owner, worked on her laptop at the patio table. She sipped a soda and read aloud every now and then. She had pretty blue eyes with dark blond hair and freckles. Her lips were glossy and pink, and her teeth were straight and white. The heels of her tan cowboy boots scraped lightly on the table as she propped her feet up and looked across the lawn at Ruby and me.

"Hi, my handsome king. Hi, my beautiful queen. What

would I do without you guys?"

"Hello," screeched Sam, Jenny's parrot, who perched happily on the back of her chair.

Jenny giggled at Sam and waved to us. She took a drink of her soda and went back to typing.

"So, do you think I'm her favorite dog yet?" I asked Ruby, who lounged on a patch of dirt where a doghouse once sat.

"Not a chance," Ruby answered with confidence.

As I went to lay my head down, I glanced toward the house and swore I saw two figures dancing inside the parlor. Before I could blink, the woman waved to me and tossed her head back in laughter. *Impossible*, I thought. Nobody was home except for us. Larry was at work, and the kids were at school. When I looked up again, they were gone.

"What is it, Byron?" asked Ruby.

"Oh, nothing," I said. "I must have been dreaming."

Just then, a cool wind blew past my ears and into the reeds. "I love you, Thor," whispered the tall grasses as they swayed in the wind. And then they were still.

"I love you, too," I whispered back.

I was home.

The real story
of Byron

On October 2, 2004 my grandmother, Trudy Charron, passed away. She was eighty-nine years old and had been sick with myasthenia gravis and emphysema. She was smart, witty, and charming, and had the tenacity of a soldier. I admired my grandma like no one else and continue to rely on her strength to this day. I loved her dearly and will miss her always.

As a young couple in the 1940s, my grandparents chose to raise their family in the country to escape the threat of a nuclear attack on Detroit. Clare Charron was my grandpa, and they had four children, two of whom were mentioned in the story. Julie is my mother. The deceased son was the second oldest child who died at age twenty-six. For over twenty years, the family lived in a white farmhouse in Oxford, Michigan, with a pond, a chicken coop, and a kennel for their dogs. They had a home-built doghouse where their favorite dogs slept, one of which was Thor. By far, he was the most loved German shepherd of my grandmother's. She bought him as a puppy in 1960 and raised him for five years before she decided to give him up. At that time, my grandpa forbade her to take a dog to their new house in the suburbs. Rather than fighting to keep Thor, my grandma abided and left him in the care of the new owners. Only once or twice did she visit him after that. But her visits were so painful, for both her and Thor, that she stopped going to see him. For the rest of her life, my grandma regretted her decision. Every time she mentioned Thor, it was with tears. She told that story until the day she died.

Two months after her death, I got a call from my best friend Anna Olech. Anna is a beautiful, smart person, originally from Poland, who has dedicated her life to homeless dogs. She held an adoption show at Catherine's Pet Parlor and called me to say that a big, beautiful German shepherd had just walked in and needed a home. Adena and Jeff Hejl, clients of Catherine's, had rescued him just the day before, and when they took him to Catherine's for a bath, she suggested they bring him to Anna's adoption show. So they did. Believing in miracles and connecting Anna's phone call to my grandma, I agreed to meet Byron. Later that day I brought him home, and I've loved him ever since.

I am unsure of Byron's entire history, but he seemed badly neglected. He was twenty pounds underweight, and every rib showed. I was told that he spent his entire life in a crate in a garage. In fact, he probably had less freedom in real life than he did in my story. It was also true that his previous owner was a policeman. The family had separated in divorce, and neither party wanted Byron.

Adena and Jeff heard about Byron through a mutual friend. In the end, they would have kept him if they hadn't found a good owner. But we all got lucky, and as only God knows, everything happens for a reason. I believe that, no matter what, Byron and I would have found each other.

The day he came to live with us, he brought with him a bag of food and a pink rubber ball that squeaked.

Trudy Charron in 1959.

Clare and Trudy Charron outside of their home in Oxford, MI in 1965, just before their move to Bloomfield Hills, MI.

Thor at Christmas time at the house in Oxford, MI, 1960.

The Ward family one week after acquiring Byron. Jennifer, holding Jackie with Sam on shoulder and Byron to her right; Larry, with Henry on shoulder and Ruby to his left; Josie and Jake below. (Byron was actually photoshopped in later—he was too disruptive to take to the initial photo shoot.)

Byron, 18 months old, with his original pink ball in the Wards'
backyard.

Anna Olech with Wolfie (left) and Alex (right).

Photo by Anna Olech 2008

Author Biography

Jennifer Charron Ward was born and raised in Birmingham, Michigan. She grew up with two dogs and a cat and inherited her love of animals from both her mother and father. She earned her Bachelor of Science in Microbiology from the University of Michigan-Dearborn. She then went on to complete her Master of Science in Physician Assistant Studies at the University of Detroit Mercy. Jennifer met her husband Larry in 1989, got Ruby in 1992, and married Larry in 1993. Since then, they have had Jake and Josie, and many non-human children including Byron. The Ward family resides in Oakland County, Michigan. *Running Home* is Jennifer's first book.